Axel was on his feet, tail wagging as he barked.

Turning to look at Willow, Carter felt his chest tighten.

Her eyes were alight with pleasure and she wore a beautiful smile as she gazed at Axel. She did adore dogs. Or this one anyway. "Hello, fella. How're you doing?" She bent down to pat the pup as he pushed up against her, his nose pressed into her thigh.

They looked as though they'd always known each other, as if they belonged together. "You're a perfect match," Carter said through the sudden yearning to be a part of the picture.

"You don't give up, do you?"

"Nope." That was a lie. He'd given up on a lot of things the day Cassandra turned her back on him.

"What do you think, Axel?" Willow was running her hand down the pup's back, and the way Axel arched into her touch said he was more than happy to spend more time with her.

"Do you really have to ask?" Carter concentrated on the here and now. Which included Willow Taylor. Something ab___ ___ ___ked his interest…

Dear Reader,

They say that opposites attract and vet Carter and vet nurse Willow could not be more opposite if they tried. Except for one thing. Their pasts are painful and keeping them from diving into a new and exciting relationship.

They want each other, but Willow never stops long anywhere, and Carter is not leaving the Gold Coast to follow her. He's settled there, while she doesn't look like she's settling any time soon, if at all.

Follow these two as they overcome their fears and accept their love for each other. It's not easy, but nothing this important ever is.

I loved writing a story set on the Gold Coast of Australia, where it's warm and the beaches amazing, the people so friendly. I hope you enjoy a glimpse into this lifestyle.

Cheers,

Sue MacKay

www.SueMacKay.co.nz
suemackayauthor@mail.com

BROUGHT TOGETHER BY A PUP

———

SUE MacKAY

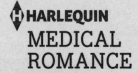

HARLEQUIN

MEDICAL
ROMANCE

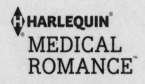

HARLEQUIN®
MEDICAL ROMANCE™

PLEASE RECYCLE

Recycling programs
for this product may
not exist in your area.

ISBN-13: 978-1-335-73778-6

Brought Together by a Pup

Harlequin Enterprises ULC
22 Adelaide St. West, 41st Floor
Toronto, Ontario M5H 4E3, Canada
www.Harlequin.com

Printed in U.S.A.

Sue MacKay lives with her husband in New Zealand's beautiful Marlborough Sounds, with the water on her doorstep and the birds and the trees at her back door. It is the perfect setting to indulge her passions of entertaining friends by cooking them sumptuous meals, drinking fabulous wine, going for hill walks or kayaking around the bay—and, of course, writing stories.

Books by Sue MacKay

Harlequin Medical Romance

Queenstown Search & Rescue

Captivated by Her Runaway Doc
A Single Dad to Rescue Her
From Best Friend to I Do?

The Nurse's Secret
The GP's Secret Baby Wish
Their Second Chance in ER
Fling with Her Long-Lost Surgeon
Stranded with the Paramedic
Single Mom's New Year Wish

Visit the Author Profile page
at Harlequin.com for more titles.

CHAPTER ONE

'WILLOW, I'VE PUT you down as my partner for the wedding.'

The overly confident voice of her friend's brother filled the car.

Couldn't be.

Willow checked the screen of her phone. She'd stopped for a coffee on the way home after a weekend at Noosa in anticipation of Pip's wedding. Now this.

Definitely Dr Dave Greenslade calling. She shuddered. The last man she wanted anything to do with. This side of her ninetieth birthday anyway. She'd heard stories from one of the bridesmaids about his wandering hands. He hadn't asked her to be his partner, just told her, as though she should be grateful he'd take her since she had a disability. Arrogance personified was Dave. Didn't matter. She wasn't accepting his plan.

She still had to sit at the same table on the

day, so she'd better play a little bit nice, for Pip's sake. 'Thanks, but I don't need a partner.' Not him anyway. His attitude of 'I'm so important' had rubbed her up the wrong way the few times she'd seen him.

'Come on. You don't want to go on your own. You'll look better hanging off my arm. Everyone who means anything will be there.'

Count her out, then. She wasn't going just to be 'noticed'. Anyway, he was exaggerating, because most of Pip's friends were nurses at the Gold Coast Hospital, regular people. 'Again, no thanks,' she said through gritted teeth.

'You think you're going to get a better offer this close to the wedding? When you don't know many decent people on the Gold Coast and I'm offering? You can't do better than that. Think of who I am.' His ego wasn't taking being turned down.

Fury began to bubble up her throat. To hell with the dirt bag. 'I'll look just fine.' Walking in on her own or with her hand slipped through some man's arm, she'd make sure of it. After this one's smart-mouthed comments she was going to find a partner, even if she had to pay him. No one put her down. No one. 'I'll see you there.'

And turn my back on you when I do.

'Looking forward to it.' Dave sounded peeved.

'We'll wave as we dance past,' she added for good measure. He'd made her mad. She'd hazard a bet that he'd come up with the idea of asking her because no one else would go with him. She smiled.

'We? Thought you didn't have a partner? Make up your mind, Willow. I wouldn't have thought you'd find someone suitable so easily.'

'Bye, Dave.' She stabbed the off button. Stuck-up egotist who believed he was the best cardiologist in Australia. Unfortunately, rumour said he might be right. Obviously he hadn't taken a course about learning to be compassionate. Hard to believe he grew up in the same family as Pippa. Except she might be behind that call, having occasionally hinted Willow should go out with Dave. She hadn't been keen before; after that conversation he didn't stand a chance.

She was seething as she pulled back out onto the road. So what if she had a prosthetic lower leg? Along with the deep scarring on her upper arm and shoulder, she wasn't the prettiest girl on the block, but did that matter? It didn't make her unacceptable amongst people, or hadn't so far, any rate. Apart from the last man she'd set out to have a bit of fun with who hadn't been able to look at her leg when she'd removed the prosthesis to have sex. His look of disgust had reiterated a big lesson she'd learned after the accident. Not to let anyone who wouldn't take her as she was get close. They didn't deserve the effort. She was worth a lot more than them.

She had three weeks to find a man who might not mind how she limped because no way in hell would she let Dave think he was right.

Willow, you moron. You said we, as in you'd have a partner. When there isn't even a hint of a man in your life.

She'd taken a break from getting back into the dating game since the last mistake. She didn't give a brass razoo about what other people thought of her false leg. It got her from A to B, made her capable of continuing in the career she adored working with animals, and kept her independent. 'So, Greenslade, go bite yourself somewhere it hurts.' Turning off the highway, she headed onto a secondary road.

'Who are you going to find to go to the wedding with?' an annoying little voice in the back of her head demanded.

There was the problem. The men she'd

worked with in her last job were all in relationships, which was probably why she got on with them so well. They posed no threats to her sometimes fragile outward determination to be treated equally to everyone else. There might be someone available at the vet clinic she was starting at on Wednesday, but the chances were slim. It didn't leave her a lot of time to suss anyone out enough. She did like to know a little about who she dated, just to be safe.

'Whoa. Look out.' Willow swerved to avoid a dog half standing, half sprawled at the side of the road.

Braking, she glanced in the rear-vision mirror. The animal hadn't moved. Parking on the verge, she got out and, ignoring the stabs of pain the prosthesis sent to her knee, jogged unevenly back to the dog, which was whining pitifully. The pain-filled eyes watching her approach snagged her heart and sucked her in. A quick glance told her it was a male. Plus his feet were big for his size indicating he was a puppy, possibly about ten months old.

'What's up, little fella?'

He was shaking hard, as though afraid, but the vet nurse in her suspected shock to be the stronger reason—and pain. Given where he was and how his back leg was tucked underneath his belly, it was more than likely that he'd been hit by a vehicle. He needed help, and he was going to get it.

An ache she always tried to ignore began deep inside. If she stopped wandering the world she could have love, whether from a four-footed male or one with two feet firmly on the ground, either would give her a new perspective on life. One she wasn't ready for. Being continuously on the move left little time to reflect on the past and the tragedy that had altered her for ever, and that was how she liked it.

Crouching down on her good knee, she slowly reached one hand out for the pup to sniff. 'What happened? Did you get hit by a car?' At the end of the working day this road was busy with people keen to get home to their beachfront properties, or, in her case, the air-conditioned house three streets away from Main Beach in Southport she'd moved into six months ago when she came to the Gold Coast to work a temporary position at another vet clinic. She shared it with two women, one a pilot, the other a beauty therapist.

When the dog, likely a Huntaway, let her pat his head, she slowly began moving her hands over his neck and down his back, chest, and finally to the rear leg he held at an unnatural angle, making soothing sounds as she went. Every touch was slow and gentle, so as not to frighten or hurt, nor get bitten for her trouble. 'There you go. I think you've dislocated your hip, fella. I'm a vet nurse, in case you're doubting me. You need to see a vet.'

She'd go straight to Rural and Suburban Veterinary Clinic in Southport where her next contract started the day after tomorrow. It wasn't far and she might be able to help with this fella, something she wanted to do as those sad eyes sucked her in deeper and deeper with every agonised breath he took.

At the car, she opened the back door before limping back to lift the dog off the roadside. Dang but he was heavy for a pup. Her back protested. Which was nothing to what her right leg was doing as she teetered towards the car. Tough. She was not dropping him. No way. The pain would be unbearable for him. As it was, he was whimpering full on, which got faster and louder when she made it to the car and leaned in awkwardly to place him on the back seat. 'There you go.'

After giving him another rub over his head and ears, she went around to the front seat and got in, ignoring the ache in her leg muscles from all the driving she'd been doing over the last few days. A lot of groaning was going on in the back. 'I'm onto it. Lie as still as you can for a few more minutes.'

He answered with a low moan.

'It's going to be all right. Promise.' Wrong thing to say. She knew better than to make promises she mightn't be able to keep. Her well and truly *ex*-boyfriend had promised she'd be fine after the accident that cost her the lower half of her right leg and two close friends who died at the scene. That was before he'd learned about the amputation. When he had, he'd taken one look, said he couldn't cope and gone home to pack his bags. But this pup was going to be fine, though he did look as though he could do with a few decent feeds as his ribs were too obvious. 'What's your story, fella?'

Another moan.

'I should've learnt to speak dog.'

Won't be necessary, Willow. The vet will find he's been chipped, the owner's name will become apparent and he can be reunited with those who love him.

'Lucky boy,' she sighed. Not that she couldn't return home to Sydney and her family whenever she wanted. Any time the wanderlust backed off, that was, which wasn't on the horizon yet, if it ever would be. Certainly not before the memories of those two friends who'd died and all they were missing out on had receded to the back of her mind and she could face life without feeling guilty she could still make plans and be happy.

Five minutes later she pulled up outside an ordinary-looking single-storey building with a large sign telling her she'd found the veterinary clinic right where she'd believed it was. Even better, there were lights on inside, which probably meant that it had been a busy day since it was now seven o'clock—and Monday night. 'You stay there while I go get us some help.' Not that there was much chance of him moving unaided.

The pup continued to whimper.

Her heart tightened and had her leaning between the seats to pat her passenger. 'This is the best place for you right now. Someone's going to make you all good again.' They'd better or they'd have her to answer to. She'd been interviewed online by one of the vets, Joe, and he'd come across as genuinely compassionate about animals in need of treatment. Okay, like most vets she'd worked with. Still, hopefully it would be him inside.

It took a lot of knocking and buzzer pressing before the door finally swung open and a tall, unshaven man with tired eyes and drooping shoulders stood in front of her. 'Yes?'

Not Joe, the vet who'd interviewed her online. 'Are you a vet?'

'I am.'

'I have a puppy in my car I think might've been hit by a vehicle. I found him on the side of the road a way back.' She inclined her head towards her car. 'I'm Willow Taylor, by the way.'

'I'll come take a look.' He shoved a stopper under the door to keep it from closing and followed her to the car.

Her name hadn't registered. A new vet nurse, temporary at that, obviously wasn't the most important thing on his mind. 'It's my pick his hip's dislocated.' She opened the door. 'Here you go, fella. This man's a vet.'

The vet leaned in and did much the same to reassure the puppy as she had earlier before touching the hip. After a couple of minutes, he straightened. 'Let's get him inside.'

'It's not going to be easy extricating him from the car. I didn't think about that when I put him on the back seat. Not that I had a lot of choice.' She went to the front and pulled the seat forward, allowing a little more space for those wide shoulders.

'I've got him,' the man said and straightened slowly with the dog in his arms. 'Follow me.'

Yes, sir.

She hadn't been about to disappear before finding out more about the injuries and where the dog's owner was anyway. Pinging the locks on her car, she went inside and closed the door when told. The way the orders rolled off his tongue the guy probably had a brood of kids at home he was used to issuing instructions to.

'Hopefully he's microchipped,' she said to the straight back she was following.

'I'll check shortly. First he needs pain relief. Then I'll see what the problem is. The way he's favouring his hip says it is a dislocation, but there might also be fractures. There's also something wrong with his paw.'

This was sounding a lot like the accident she'd had years back. More and more coming to light as the minutes went by and medics poked and prodded. 'Will you amputate if there's no hope of a fracture healing?' she asked even when she knew the answer, her mind going back to her accident.

'Depends on a lot of things.'

Didn't she know it? 'I suppose.' One option was euthanasia, the other a badly deformed leg to run around on for ever. The only option she'd faced when the truck had crashed through the group of cyclists she was part of and run over her lower leg was to lose the lower half of that limb. Her ex, Gavin, had tried to deal with what happened, but couldn't manage it. He had still broken her heart, even when it was already busted over the deaths of her friends.

Following the vet into a procedure room, Willow watched him place the dog ever so carefully on the table. His gentleness made her blink, even though she'd seen it often in the many clinics she'd worked at. His four-footed patients must adore him. And she'd bet the humans in his life did. She moved to the top of the table and ran her hand over the pup's head, back and forth, to keep him calm.

Again pain-filled eyes met hers and a low whine sent chills down her spine. 'Shh. You're going to be okay.'

He'd better be. She'd promised. The trust in his eyes was undoing her resolve to remain aloof. But he'd have an owner. She was leaving in eight weeks.

Sorry, boyo, but I'm not the one for you.

The vet studied his patient, professionalism all over his face and in his gaze.

Willow studied *him* from under lowered eyelids, not so professionally. His well-worn jeans fitted perfectly, while the wrinkled shirt did little to hide honed upper-arm and chest muscles. Not that she was in the market for a man. Not even the idea of a short fling got her all hot and twitchy these days. She only had to remember the look on the face of the last man she'd dated when they'd got down and dirty in her bed to know she wasn't ready to completely expose her imperfect body to another one any time soon.

Those fingers touching, pressing, soothing the animal were long and strong, and evoked memories of being made love to by Gavin in the days before the transport truck jackknifed into the cyclists' path and changed her life for ever. What a nightmare that ride had turned into, a nightmare that hadn't gone away since. Willow swallowed, and concentrated on the sad little guy she'd rescued from the side of the road and how the vet would get him back up and running around, tail wagging.

'I suspect he was injured at least a day ago, if not more. There's too much muscle stiffness for it to have happened in the past few hours. I'll X-ray his hip, then decide what to do next.' He turned his intense gaze on her as though she were in need of his help as much as the dog. How untrue. 'I'm Carter Adams, by the way.'

In case he'd missed it the first time she told him, 'I'm Willow. I start working here on Wednesday.'

His eyes widened. 'Welcome to the clinic, Willow. Not quite how you'd have expected your first time with us to be, I imagine.'

'Can't say it was, but when I found the pup I figured I might as well bring him here. Though you might've preferred I went elsewhere so you could go home. You look like you've had a big day.' When his forest-green eyes widened further, she muttered, 'Just saying it how I see it.' Those eyes were intense.

'Right.' He turned to the pup. 'I'll get on with this.'

Thankfully, she'd be back on the road any minute and this interlude of insanity over a pair of eyes would be a brief blip in her memory. By tomorrow she'd have gathered her scattered brain and put it under control so come Wednesday it would be as though she'd never met him and could start with a clean slate. Then she opened her mouth and blurted, 'Do you want a hand?' So her brain was on autopilot. She was always offering to help whenever she thought she might be useful. Maybe this was a dream and any second she'd wake up and have a darned good laugh at herself.

'He seems comfortable with you so, yes, it would help if you remained with us for a while to keep him settled.'

With us. Sounded good. They wouldn't be total strangers when she turned up on Wednesday. Then again, so what? She was used to strangers in her life, what with only working temporary positions and moving towns on a regular basis, so half an hour in Carter's company wouldn't change any of that. 'You're on.' Turning to their patient, she returned to petting him. The other male in the room was quite something. Good-looking for sure. Especially with that chin and the stubble. Nothing like stubble rubbing against her palm.

Don't you need a date for the wedding?

So what? She was hardly going to blurt that out. She wouldn't get to even start the job on Wednesday. But he could be a contender. She'd take her time and find out if he was as decent as he came across with the pup. Good looks meant nothing if not backed up with a kind and caring personality. He'd been all of that with the pup, not so much with her. More like aloof, or plain couldn't give a toss about her other than as a vet nurse.

Which was how he should be. That *was* her role here, nothing more.

Carter ignored the hot vibes emanating from the woman on the other side of the table where the dog lay quiet under her soothing hands. A bitzer. Not her; the pup. Mostly Huntaway with some retriever thrown into the mix by the look of him. *She* was pedigree. Fine features, sharp eyes—and tongue— with a slight body. She had a serious limp, her right leg not up to scratch. Permanent or temporary injury? It was anyone's guess. He wasn't asking. He knew his boundaries. Anyway, he had a job to do getting this sorry animal back up and about. Maybe not running, but hobbling would be a good start. Then he could finally finish up for the day. He was going to get to know this woman a little better later on in the week over other surgeries and then this unusual pique of interest would fizzle away.

'Hold him while I administer a tranquilliser. I don't want to rely on either of us keeping him still while I examine him. Strange noises and people could agitate him further.' She'd be used to that, but he couldn't keep quiet round her. It was almost as though talking would keep her at a distance. He might be doing a lot of talking over the coming months if that was the case, but he doubted it. He really wasn't interested in looking further. 'Pup mightn't move, but he's already had enough shocks for one day.' Again, he wasn't saying anything she wouldn't know. Obviously the hectic day had caught up.

Empathy filled her face. 'No problem.' Firm hands with perfectly manicured nails painted with a blue that matched her eyes held the dog's lower quarters. Was she understanding the dog's situation from a personal point of view? Something to do with why she limped? Again, he wasn't asking.

As soon as he'd finished administering the drug, Carter dispensed the needle into the hazard bin and set up the overhead radiology equipment, all the time strangely aware of his companion. The human one. The animal situation was something he was used to so was no distraction. Though tonight was proving an exception to that; distraction seeming to be the way of things with his helper here in the same air he was breathing. Concentration was required and then he'd soon have the job done and the woman would leave.

Yet he couldn't help asking, 'Have you got a dog? You're very good with this one.'

'No, I don't have any pets.'

That wasn't a good look in his book. Pets were wonderful for making people's days brighter more than almost anything or anyone else did. Though this woman was gentle and understanding with the dog she'd brought in so she could be redeemed. 'You'd be the first vet nurse I've met who doesn't have a dog or cat.'

'I only came to the Gold Coast for eight months. It wouldn't have been fair to take on a dog then leave him when I move away.'

'You could always take it with you.'

'I came here from Singapore, and I'm not sure where I'm headed next.'

Her accent was dinkum Aussie. 'Where are you from originally?' He hadn't read her CV. Joe had said she ticked all the boxes more than well, so he and Seamus had gone along with the recommendation to give her the job. It was only temporary after all, two months wasn't long unless she turned out to be useless, and so far she appeared more than competent.

'Sydney. In the burbs.' She leaned over the pup and touched his head. 'How you doing, fella?' Her eyes were fixed on the animal, gone from looking at him.

The dog didn't move. Out for the count.

'He's good to go.' Whereas his helper appeared uncomfortable with him asking about personal info. It was a good thing he knew when to shut up or he might be without an assistant for the next half-hour or so.

Five minutes later, Carter stepped away from the images on the screen. 'The sacro-iliac joint is dislocated, no fractures to be seen. I'll position the joint back in place with a synthetic ligament to maintain it in situ while he starts walking again. He'll have to take things easy for about six weeks. Here's hoping his owner is good with that. Let's get ready.'

Willow took the smock he handed her and slipped her arms into it. When she reached up to button the smock in place at the back of her neck, superb curves filled the front of the dull blue fabric.

Carter swung the X-ray out of the way. Working alongside her was going to be interesting. Soft hands were soothing the pup's head, even though the animal was unaware of anything going on. He shoved away an errant image of those hands on his skin, and got on with the job of helping his patient.

Willow looked up at him, tiredness coming off her in waves now. 'What about his paw? It looks messy. At least it's not bleeding, though if he was injured days ago he's probably licked it clean.'

'A deep cut that requires suturing, but again, no fractures.' Carter prepared the induction agent. About to ask the nurse to hold the dog's shoulder while he administered the drug that would keep the animal sedated, he paused.

Her hands were already firmly in place, keeping their patient still. Once again her focus was entirely on the dog. Nothing else seemed to matter. Nor should it. The pup was his only concern too, even if it was a little hard to ignore such a lovely woman standing so near. He swallowed. It shouldn't be. It was what he did with most women, near or far. He took no notice of them. As simple as that. Except this one oozed sexiness, and a kindness also emanated from her, which he suspected might not be only for animals in need.

It didn't make any difference. He wasn't into relationships, short or long term. A fling here and there was fine, but there was no room for love in his heart. There'd only been one love of his life. Cassandra. They'd known each other most of their lives, gone to school together, got together as boyfriend and girlfriend at the age of fifteen and been inseparable ever since. When they had begun planning their wedding five years ago both families had been stoked. The day of their wedding had been sunny and warm, the spring flowers blooming as though they'd been set up to open wide on that particular day. Nothing could go wrong. Or so he'd thought until two hours before he was due at the altar.

Cass had driven up to his parents' house to talk to him, dressed not in a flowing gown but in jeans and tee shirt, her hair tied in a messy ponytail, her eyes underscored with dark shadows. His gut was taking a dive and his heart dying even before she told him she was leaving him, leaving home, and going to live in England. Put simply, she was jilting him.

'Have you fixed many dislocations?' A low voice intruded upon his dour memories.

'Um, yes, it's quite common, though just as often because of arthritis as trauma. How's he going?'

'Probably dreaming about a big bone.' She pinched a paw.

The dog didn't move or make a sound.

'Let's get this done.' Picking up a scalpel, Carter made a quick incision to insert the synthetic ligament designed to keep the joint capsule in place. As he rotated the joint he could sense the woman watching him.

Relax. I know what I'm doing.

'Sorry, I wasn't doubting you.' A pink shade flared in her tanned cheeks.

He'd spoken aloud? Hell. That was *not* a good look in front of the new nurse. It was probably because it had been a busy day that had left him feeling shattered. 'Pass me that bowl, would you?'

'Sure.' She didn't have to ask which one or where from. She must've been sussing out the room and gear while he dealt with the pup.

Despite himself, he smiled. And softened on the inside. It was such a new sensation he couldn't help smiling some more. It felt good. As if a load was beginning to fall away from where it had been lodged for years. But that couldn't be right. Half an hour ago he hadn't known this woman existed. The fact she was joining the clinic didn't mean he was about to become interested in her.

Once he'd completed putting the pup back together, he scanned for a microchip then put the number he found into the database. 'Name's Axel. He's ten months old.' Noting the address of his owner, he lifted the pup and took him through to a cage for the night.

After chucking his scrub top in the laundry basket, he told his helper, 'I'll let dog control know he's here shortly. Would you like a coffee first?'

'Sounds good. I'll order some dinner to pick up after I leave here.' Her smile showed exhaustion and her cheeks were a little pale. As for that limp, it seemed worse than when she'd first knocked on the door.

He still wasn't asking. Instead he said, 'There's a reasonable pizza place two doors down I can recommend. I often use them.' In the kitchen area he opened a drawer and handed her the menu. 'Take a look.'

'Cheers.'

As she perused the menu, he made instant coffee and pushed a mug in her direction. 'There you go.'

'Thanks.' A woman of few words, it seemed.

The front door burst open. 'Carter, what's going on? I've been ringing and leaving messages and you haven't got back to me once. Everyone's waiting for you.' Yvette stormed into the room and came to an abrupt halt. 'Oh, I see. I bet you were going to say you'd been held up by an animal needing your attention.' Her fiery eyes locked on Willow.

Forgetting to let Yvette know he'd be late for his business partner's birthday dinner was bad. He got it. But she needed to calm down. 'As a matter of fact, I have been treating a dog that's been in an accident.'

Willow intervened before Yvette could shout any more nonsense. 'I found Axel on the side of the road and brought him here.'

Yvette smirked. 'Sure you did. Think I believe that? Look at the two of you all cosy with coffees and poring over the pizza menu for dinner. Thanks, Carter. You really are an arse. Joe's wondering what's going on.'

He hadn't been standing within two metres of the menu or the woman holding it. 'Hold on, Yvette. This is Willow. She's starting with us this week. Joe interviewed her last Monday.'

Willow placed her mug on the bench, along with the menu, and headed for the door. 'I'll get on my way. See you Wednesday. Bye.' The door closed firmly behind her.

Which made it perfectly obvious she wasn't staying to clear the air between him and Yvette. Not that he could blame her. It wasn't her problem. He and Yvette had organised a surprise evening for Joe to celebrate his thirtieth birthday, and yet the moment Willow had turned up with the dog, he'd all but forgotten about it. Which showed how much she'd screwed with his mind. That hadn't happened in for ever. Nor was it happening again. 'I'll go clean myself up and change and meet you there.'

'Get a move on, will you? The hours are flying past.' Yvette was in a right mood, which wasn't unusual lately. She and Joe were having a few difficulties in their relationship, which would be adding to her stress right now. She wanted tonight to go well in the hope it could lay to rest some of the tension between her and Joe. 'I'll wait for you.'

'Sorry I got held up. I should've been in touch to let you know. Once I started working on Axel's injuries everything else went out of my mind.' He wasn't telling her he had forgotten most things when he'd opened the door to find the woman holding the dog in her arms. It was unlike him, and really told him he was an idiot. 'As you well know, this is what sometimes happens in our line of work. I'm a vet because I care about animals and helping them recover from injuries or illnesses. I can't walk away and come back in the morning to put them out of their misery. Joe's the same.'

She slumped. 'I messed up by charging in here like that, didn't I? You seemed very comfortable with her. I didn't even know you were employing a new nurse. Joe said nothing about it. Willow, did you say?'

'Yes. She's filling in while Abbie's away.' No, he hadn't been comfortable around the new nurse when they'd stopped working. That was when the unwanted sensations of interest had started up. He'd managed to quickly squash them. Not that he was saying any of this to Yvette. She'd be telling Joe the moment they got to the restaurant, probably as something to get him listening to her. Carter headed for the locker, where a clean shirt and trousers always hung in case he got caught out just like this.

'There was a spark in your eyes I haven't seen in a long time.'

Give me a break. As if. Willow was nice, all right. Nothing more.

'Go back to the restaurant. I'll be right behind you. Promise.' He did not need any of his friends hinting at the idea he might find a woman to become interested in. They'd be wasting their time and he'd be annoyed at them for hoping. Never again would he hand over his heart. If Cassandra couldn't step up beside him to say 'I do' when they knew each other so well, then he doubted there was another woman he'd want to take a chance on.

'No more animals to rescue tonight, Carter.' Yvette wagged her finger at him. At last she was smiling, tightly but a vast improvement on the angry face that had stormed through the door minutes ago. 'But if she were to return, bring her along.'

Willow. Her name is Willow, not she.

'Get out of here.' Carter tried not to smile too but one was already breaking across his face as he thought about Willow.

'See you in ten.'

'Fifteen.' He glanced out into the car park as Yvette opened the door but the only vehicle in sight was hers. No sign of Willow's car. What was he thinking? Willow might look lovely, but she hadn't acted as though she was in a hurry to get to know him any further. Something he was grateful for. She hadn't even said she'd phone him to find out how the pup was doing. He could breathe again.

Carter laughed as he checked on Axel to see how he was recovering before turning off the lights and heading out to his ute. If he had an over-inflated ego, it had just been dented, for which he should be grateful. A few hours with his friends would rein in these off-limits thoughts about a gorgeous woman who no doubt had a full life and didn't need a pathetic vet wondering if she was single and available for a date. Was Willow single?

An oath filled the air. Who cared? Not him.

CHAPTER TWO

'AXEL'S MISSING YOU,' Carter told Willow when she rang the vet clinic at what she hoped was a busy time for him the next day. 'He whines whenever anyone goes into the room where he's caged and then looks woebegone when it's not you.'

So much for not speaking to Carter. When she'd asked the receptionist about Axel she'd been put through to him whether she wanted to be or not. 'You're presuming a lot. He's more likely looking for his owner.' She hadn't spent *that* much time with the animal when he was awake.

'There's the problem. His owner's in hospital and likely to remain there for at least another ten days. She was in a serious car accident on Saturday. Axel had disappeared by the time people realised he had been in the car too. No one had seen him until you found him a good two days later.'

The poor fella. He must've been beside himself with pain and fear with his owner not there for him. 'That explains why the injuries weren't fresh. Is there other family to take care of him?'

'No. The owner, Mrs Burnside, reluctantly agreed for him to go into a boarding kennel until she's home again, but so far Dog Rescue haven't been able to find one prepared to take him. Don't ask me why. I'm only repeating what our receptionist, Kathy, was told.'

'Can he stay at the clinic?' She thought the answer was obvious, but what else could she say? It seemed Axel was caught between a rock and a hard place.

'Not for that long. You wouldn't think of looking after him?'

Here we go. Pile on the pressure, why didn't he? 'Like I said last night, I'm not here for the long term so I'm not set up for taking in a pup even for a few days.' She wasn't going to mention how her heart had softened over Axel being alone, his owner not able to be with him when he was hurting. She kind of understood where he was at. Plus, he was so cute. Those sad eyes that had followed her every move in the clinic last night until he'd succumbed to the painkiller had stuck with her ever since.

Along with another pair of eyes, though not sad ones. Eyes that she did not need following her into sleep. They'd got to her, kept reminding her she required a partner for the wedding if she was to avoid Dave's overbearing gestures. It wouldn't be Carter. He already had a woman in his life. Yvette had made it clear she was not happy to find him having coffee with her.

'We've got everything you'd need here at the clinic.' The man pulled no punches.

Not that she was surprised. Last night had shown her a man who would do anything to make his patients well and happy. Not so much the women in his life. But he'd have an agenda when it came to sad animals. Get their tails wagging again. 'You think it would be fair on Axel to come and stay with me when I won't be at home most days of the week?' She'd love to have him there and watch him get back on his feet so he could go for walks. But then she'd get too close and it would hurt to return him to his owner. One day she might settle down, but it was unlikely she'd ever have a pet. Losing it would be painful and bring back a lot of memories about her friends, Dee and Jess, who'd died.

'You could bring him in to work with you. There's usually a couple of cages going spare.

It would be a lot better for him than staying at the rescue centre where he'd have to share the love being handed around. If they take him at all.'

Like she said, this man knew how to find a person's soft spot. Hers, anyway. She refused to buy into it. 'My first, and only, question was, how's he doing?'

'Apart from missing his rescuer, he's good. He tried putting weight on his bung leg but quickly lifted it off the ground. Still, I don't think it will be long before he's running around on it. With a limp, but walking none-theless. He is a puppy after all.'

They'd make a matching pair with their limps if they went for walks. Hopefully Axel's would vanish with time and exercise. 'I'll call in later to see him.'

What was it about Carter that her usually clear mind went cloudy around him? Surpris-ing since she'd become a dab hand at avoid-ing getting close to anyone—and pets—since the loss of her friends. She would see out a contract and move on. That was the way of it. Her next move might be across to Perth in Western Australia since it was one of the places in her own country she hadn't been to. There again, she wanted to visit and work in Wales and Scotland. There was also a position she'd seen advertised last week coming up in Napier, New Zealand over winter.

'By the way, Yvette feels terrible about last night. She and I had organised a surprise dinner for her husband, and she was stressed to the max worrying that Joe would think I wasn't coming. When she's like that she lets rip without thought. She said if I was talking to you to say sorry.'

'It's fine. I'm not holding a grudge.' A wee smile slid over her lips. Partner's wife, not Carter's girlfriend. That she could handle. It shouldn't make a crumb of difference. It didn't. She wasn't interested in getting closer to Carter. Except she was on the hunt for someone to take with her to the wedding. Her flatmates hadn't been very forthcoming with names last night when she'd broached the subject. 'What time do you expect to close?' She was heading to the beach shortly. Nothing like swimming in the surf to keep her muscles in shape, and her stump firm.

'Supposedly six o'clock, but that rarely happens. Regardless of the time though, I'll be here.'

So she was going to see him today. Which made her think about the wedding again. And Carter. So much for avoiding the hot dude with jeans that emphasised a muscular butt and a shirt highlighting a wide chest.

From her interview she knew there were three vets working at the clinic. Did this mean Carter was deliberately staying back so he could continue nudging her to take Axel on? From the little she'd seen he appeared to be determined when he wanted to achieve an outcome. Especially for a pup that had been found in a traumatic situation. He hadn't been focused on her. There'd nothing between them, not even a flare of interest. A small sparkle maybe. Make that definitely on her side, but Carter hadn't looked at her twice. There probably was a woman in his life. Why wouldn't there be? He was good-looking, and downright sexy in those fitted jeans, probably about thirty and settled in his own place by now. Of course he had a partner.

'I'm not sure what time I'll get there.' She could cut the beach visit short, but she didn't want to rush around looking like a besotted female when she was not interested in relationships, or even flings, since men seemed put off by her lack of a leg.

'Doesn't matter. See you whenever.' And he was gone.

Yeah, Willow. You're going to see Carter again.

To have another glimpse of a good-looking man who had managed to undermine her usual deliberate lack of interest when it came to feeling intrigued about a male. It should be an interesting few minutes at the clinic, then. Why go? Axel didn't really need her attention. Nor did Carter. But she felt driven to see him again. It was crazy when she was about to start working at the same clinic and everything would be about professionalism. Tomorrow morning to be precise.

A shiver ran down her spine. Men didn't do this to her. She didn't want them to. She was running solo and intended staying that way for a while to come. Another shiver lifted the hairs on her arms. The way she was reacting to Carter felt as though she was coming out of hibernation. The winter in her heart could not be over. Not that easily and quickly. She wasn't ready to heat up and let people in. What if another disaster happened? She doubted she'd be able to cope a second time. Let's face it, she'd barely got through the pain of last time. Two close friends gone in an ugly, terrifying blink. The image of which was seared on her brain.

Bodies everywhere. People screaming. Cycles broken. The wrecked truck looming over her, pinning down Dee. Excruciating pain. Sirens wailing. People dashing everywhere, asking questions, helping her. Saving her. Covering Dee and Jess with blankets, feet to head, nothing to be seen of their usually bright sunny faces. Ever again.

She jammed her phone in her beach bag, snatched up her keys and raced for the door. She'd swim until she couldn't lift an arm, and then she'd swim some more.

The clinic had been closed nearly half an hour when Carter glanced at his watch for the third time in five minutes. Every second seemed like an hour. What time would Willow get here? She couldn't be working somewhere else, could she? She was rostered to start here tomorrow, working with him, as it happened. Not because he'd put her name down. Kathy did the rosters and had done the nurses' days ago.

A car pulled into the parking lot out front. Willow's. The tightness in his muscles lightened. She'd come.

To see Axel, not you.

The tightness returned. She hadn't been the slightest bit interested in him last night. Nor had he been in her, or so he kept telling himself, yet he hadn't been able to stop thinking about her ever since. He should be glad for her lack of interest. They had to work together for the next two months, getting sidetracked wasn't in the interest of good working relationships. He wasn't in the market for romance, he reminded himself for the umpteenth time. He was comfortable with the slow and steady lifestyle he lived.

It had taken years to accept Cassandra was never coming back, that she'd meant it when she'd said they were too close, hadn't had enough experiences outside the rural community they'd grown up in to be settling down together in the same area. It was a valid point, but he still couldn't understand why they couldn't have done something about it—together. She'd moved on fast, was now settled with a Scotsman and about to have a baby. She'd definitely gathered more experience. He was still getting around to it, preferring to protect his heart and wait until he was absolutely certain he was ready to take a chance on love again.

It might never happen. A sad sigh escaped. When he saw how happy his two brothers were with their wives and kids he did wonder if he should try harder to move on and take a giant leap of trust. Then he'd remember his wedding day and the pain that knifed him when Cass came to call it off.

The door opened and Willow limped in, then hesitated. She looked utterly shattered, as though even breathing was hard work.

Carter's lungs stalled. Despite the exhaustion rippling off her in waves, she was gorgeous with a capital G. She wore a sleeveless pink blouse and white denim knee-length shorts. Dark scars marred her right shoulder. 'Hi. You okay?'

Defiance blinked out at him. 'Why wouldn't I be?'

Which was in complete contrast to his initial first impression. Understanding hit him. At least he thought he might be right. She was wary of his reaction to the prosthesis. She'd probably heard every kind of inane or sympathetic comment over the years and was waiting for more. He met her resigned look and said, 'Come on in. You are going to make one boy very happy.'

'Any changes since I phoned?' Willow closed the door behind her. She hadn't relaxed but she was limping forward, almost dragging her prosthesis. Damp, long thick hair the colour of milk chocolate fell across her shoulders and down her back, teasing him with the need to reach out and run his fingers through it. It was nothing like the tight knot it had been scrunched into last night.

'He's moving a little easier, but still whimpers a lot. I think that's more about being stuck in a cage with only strangers to talk to him than discomfort.' He led Willow through to the back room.

Instantly Axel was on his feet, tail wagging as he barked once.

Turning to look at Willow, Carter felt his chest tighten.

Her eyes were now alight with pleasure, and she wore a beautiful smile as she gazed at Axel. She did adore dogs. Or this one anyway. 'Hello, fella. How're you doing?' She opened the cage and bent down to pat the pup as he pushed up against her, his nose pressed into her thigh.

They looked as though they'd always known each other, even as if they belonged together. 'You're a perfect match,' Carter said through the sudden yearning to be a part of the picture.

'You don't give up, do you?'

'Nope.' That was a lie. He'd given up on a lot of things the day Cassandra turned her back on him. Plans for the future involving a family and a home to share with them, trips around the country and even possibly off-shore, to name a few. He'd stopped living.

Carter straightened, stepped back. It wasn't true. He'd been protecting himself, recovering from a broken heart, and afraid to step out into the real world again. He had not stopped living. He was a partner in this veterinary business. He had a house in South-port and a small cottage on his family's farm. He joined in everything they did, including spending plenty of hours with his nieces and nephews. He was busy all the time.

'What do you think, Axel?' Willow was running her hand down the pup's back and the way Axel arched into her touch said he was more than happy with the idea of spending more time with her.

'Do you really have to ask?' Carter pushed aside the shock of what he'd just realised about himself and concentrated on the here and now. Which included Willow Taylor. Something about her tweaked his interest. 'Are you thinking you will take him in for the days needed till his owner goes home?'

She straightened and locked formidable eyes on him. 'Mrs Burnside, Miriam, is at the Gold Coast Hospital and I called in to see her this morning. She's so grateful Axel's safe, and for the treatment you've given him. She has been trying to find someone to take him in until she's capable but it's not easy given she's in a bad way with serious injuries and using a phone tires her.'

'That was kind of you. One less thing for her to worry about, knowing Axel is safe.' Carter paused, sensing if he said any more about Willow looking after the pup she'd back off permanently. Something was causing her to hesitate. It could be as simple as trying to encourage her flatmates to agree, or it could be she didn't do getting involved with pets because she'd been upset by the loss of one.

'I think it helped her. One less worry when she's so ill.'

No doubt about it; Willow was kind-hearted. 'Feel like having that coffee we didn't get to last night? Or we could take Axel out to the yard and have a beer while he wanders around. I'm off duty, so can relax some.'

Her head flipped up, and she stared at him for a moment, as though arguing with herself.

He waited.

Finally, 'Second suggestion sounds good. Thanks.' Willow slipped through the door out into the yard, Axel at her side, not waiting for him.

He watched for a moment, taken in by that connection between Willow and the pup nudging her good knee. It wasn't the first time he'd seen a dog take to someone so fast, accepting and believing in them in a straightforward way. So much trust given so easily when it came to animals was awesome. It often happened with pets in need of being loved, though this one was already cared for. Why weren't humans like that with each other? Or were they? Was he the one with problems? Of course he had issues. Who wouldn't if they'd been hurt as he had been by Cass?

What was Willow's history? Did she have a partner? Probably not if she moved around as much as she'd indicated. How did she lose her lower leg? When did it happen? Questions flew around his head. Questions he wasn't about to put out there for her to tell him to mind his own business and storm away leaving him filled with regret. Working together should be in a comfortable environment, not one he'd turned icy by being inquisitive. He didn't need to know any more about her than her ability as a vet nurse. Learning more about her could lead to getting too close, which might take him down a path where he again got hurt.

'I'll grab the beer.' Cold and thirst-quenching liquid was what he needed, nothing else. No female distractions. He didn't do travelling around the world long term. Couldn't even consider short term now that he was tied up with the vet clinic. This was where he belonged. Willow moved around lots, so she wouldn't be staying on here after this job. He needed to keep that at the forefront of his mind and forget she was attractive along with kind.

We make a right odd pair, both limping along like a couple of has-beens, Willow thought as she walked around the yard with Axel. He didn't seem to want to leave her side for a minute, not even to go ten metres to the far wall.

What did Carter think about her prosthesis? Because there was bound to be something going on inside that craggy head. He didn't seem to be someone who missed anything, and her physical state was pretty damned obvious, especially tonight after her swim. She'd flung her togs off and pulled on a shirt and knee-length shorts without much thought. She wasn't even trying to make it look less obvious because it was a way of dampening down the strange awakening in her body. When he really took on board her disfigured body, he wouldn't look at her twice.

Anyway, no matter what, she was heading away again. It was how she managed to survive her heartbreak and avoid any more. If only she didn't feel this awakening within her—as though she'd found something she'd been deliberately avoiding for years.

Carter sat at the outdoor table by the fence, sipping from a bottle. This vague attraction to him hadn't faded overnight. He was good-looking and tall and well honed. There were plenty of good-looking, fit men out there she'd not taken a second look at so why did this one in particular set her pulse racing a little faster than normal?

He had just given her the once-over, his eyes brightening for a moment as they cruised down her body. Enough of a moment to have her wondering if he was attracted to her. Okay, so she found him interesting. Interesting? Try sexy.

Even better, he hadn't come up with something inane when he'd seen her prosthesis, as others did. She understood they didn't know whether to pretend they hadn't noticed or to say something bland to get it out of the way. Carter hadn't cringed and had carried on as though nothing was out of the ordinary. Exactly how she liked people to react.

Except this time she'd hoped it would be the dampener on her emotions she needed. He had her trying to second-guess what he thought—because, if she was honest, she didn't want him turning his back on her. It was hard to understand where this came from, considering she wasn't looking for a man to become part of her life. They'd want her to settle down, not keep moving, grabbing all the dreams she'd held before her opportunities imploded and she missed out for ever.

As well as making her want to avoid further pain, Jess's and Dee's deaths had made her go and grab at life since they no longer could. She didn't want to miss out if tragedy struck her too soon as it had them. It would be a waste of her life. So she wasn't looking for a permanent relationship any time soon. She had too much to do first. Dreams to chase and make the most of. On her own. It was far safer that way.

But a fling with a handsome man who accepted her as she was? *What do you think, Jess? Dee?* She could hear them shouting, *Yes!* It couldn't hurt, surely? Not if she was aware of the restrictions on her heart. Which she most definitely was.

'Here.' Carter held out the second bottle. 'Get some of that into you.'

'Thanks.' Carefully avoiding contact with those fingers holding the bottle, she sank onto the wooden seat attached to the table and took a sip of the cold liquid. 'Just what the doctor ordered. Or should I say vet?'

'Since you're definitely human, doctor works.'

For the first time since she'd met him, she grinned. She was that relaxed. He'd noticed she was human. As in a female, with curves and boobs? Not only the fake leg? Please have noticed more than that. Damn, she shouldn't have worn this sleeveless blouse. The scars on the back of her arm were obvious to a blind man, and Carter wasn't blind. Yeah, and he was a man. A hot male responsible for the exciting spears of heat stabbing at her inside and out. Did he do short flings by any chance? Why not? Yeah, but with her?

Suddenly she saw the face of the last guy she'd been intimate with, his horror when she took the prosthesis off. As if she was meant to have sex with a chunk of titanium knocking into him? No way in hell did she want to see that look on Carter's face. She might be getting ahead of herself, but no one else was going to protect her heart. Her grin slipped. She might as well scare him off now. 'So you noticed I don't have four legs?'

'Kind of.'

Great. Now what? Could hardly say she only had one. He knew. 'Or a tail.'

A deep, sexy chuckle reached her. 'Didn't say that.'

Corny. But warming. Okay, she was going to get this out in the open so she could move past it. 'Four years ago I was run over by a truck when it jackknifed into the group of cyclists I was on a training ride with.' Funny how she hated people bringing up the subject and yet when Carter hadn't, she rushed in to tell him. What was this about? Apart from making sure he knew about her problems sooner rather than later? There was the empty seat at the wedding to fill, and he would be a perfect fit. But was it all right to ask one of her temporary bosses to accompany her?

'From what I've seen you've done well with your recovery. Nothing seems to slow you down. Did you sustain any other serious injuries?'

'A broken arm and some scarring.' She had survived. Others hadn't.

'Bet you don't sleep as easily as you once used to.' He was watching her as he sipped his beer, nothing but care in his expression. He wasn't overdoing the concern, nor was there a lot of over-eager interest for the details.

'There is that. All part of the horror that happened and never quite goes away.' Her heart softened for the first time in a long time. She could really get to like this man. If she was staying around, which she didn't intend to. She was nowhere near ready. Might never be. 'So, are you a local?'

'Born and bred on a farm near Tamborine. I live on the coast just beyond of South Port now. My brothers both went into farming, adding to Dad's property over the years. I chose to be a vet instead. I prefer making animals well, not raising them to be sent to the meat works.' He looked a bit stunned, as though he didn't usually talk about himself.

Something they had in common. 'I get that.'

'Can't be why you're a vet nurse though.'

Her turn to laugh. 'True. I'm not sure why I chose this career, really. The end of my last year at school was approaching when the science teacher had a talk with me, and said she thought I'd make a good nurse, but the time required for study didn't fit in with my cycling regime so I sort of drifted into vet nursing instead.' She'd been a road-cycling racer and making a name for herself until the crash.

'Any regrets?'

'None whatsoever. It suits me perfectly.' The teacher had read her well though. She would've enjoying human nursing. 'I get a lot of satisfaction from helping animals when they're having a terrible time with injuries or illness.'

'How do you manage to stand all day? Isn't there a lot of pressure on your knee?' He wasn't backward in asking, but it was really a technical question, so she accepted it.

Carter had a way of wording his curiosity that didn't make her want to tell him to mind his own business. Or she was more ready to listen to him than usual because he had tweaked her interest. 'It often hurts like stink, but I manage.' It was never going to be an excuse for not doing a good job. She had always maintained good relationships with her employers as she never knew when she might be back wanting another job with them.

'Sounds like you get around a lot.' Now there was a question in his eyes.

One she wasn't answering. What she said was, 'I love travelling, seeing the sights, meeting different people, and working in those places means trying to become a part of the culture for as long as I'm there.'

'The Gold Coast culture.' He laughed. 'Now that's a new one. We're all Aussies. What culture is there here?'

She laughed too. 'Surfing, prawns, lots of sunshine, crazy theme parks.'

'Sydney doesn't have those?'

'Sure it does, but the city's huge and it takes for ever to get anywhere.' Especially when she didn't ride a bike any more. Cycling had been her passion, and while it was possible to ride with her prosthesis, she would never again be a competitive cyclist, something she couldn't face.

She reached down to rub Axel between his ears. He was curled up at her feet, looking the most relaxed she'd seen him. Come to think of it, she felt more relaxed around Carter than she had with any man in a long time other than at work. Dared she invite him to the wedding? When he was one of her bosses? He could also be in a relationship, though that looked less likely now he'd offered to share a beer rather than racing home to be with someone.

Time to get out of here. Except it would be rude to leave before she finished her drink. Or walk away when Carter was nothing but friendly. Add in sexy, and kind, and non-confrontational. She might as well enjoy the moment before going home to whip up something to eat.

Ask him about the wedding, will you? Just put it out there.

What did she have to lose? It wasn't as though she was committing to anything more than a few hours in his company. Also, if he said no, then it wouldn't be a big deal either.

Commitment. It wasn't her thing. Unless it was to a job, and then only for a short time. She took a big gulp of beer. She had enjoyed the places where she'd been working, and the people she'd met. But at times she felt as though she were on a treadmill going faster and faster and struggling to keep up.

'Should I be getting on my way and letting you get home to someone?' she asked Carter in a rush. Blimey, her heart was beating something awful. Was his answer so important? When she was usually strong and took knocks on the chin easier than she did swallowing painkillers for her knee?

His eyes widened. 'Is that your way of asking if I'm single?' He was direct.

She appreciated that. 'Yes. The thing is, I'm in need of a partner for my friend's wedding and as I don't know many guys I'm a little desperate. I understand we're going to be working together so I should probably shut up about now.' What was going on? She might be tired to the bone after all that swimming, but it wasn't an excuse for acting so out of character. Next he'd be ringing Joe to say they had to tear up the contract with the nurse.

'That's the last—'

The sound of screeching brakes drowned him out. Quickly followed by screams.

'What the?' Carter was on his feet, striding to the back gate. Pulling it open, he stared down the lane. 'Willow, we're needed. There's a guy on the ground beside a car.'

Leaping to her feet, she cursed the stab of pain in her knee and raced across to join Carter as he headed onto the lane, closing the gate to keep Axel safe. 'Looks like the car hit him,' she said. Two people were already at his side, bending down, looking as though they were about to roll him over.

'Don't move him,' she called. 'He might have a spinal injury.'

Both stepped back in a hurry. 'Sorry, just thought we had to see if he's breathing,' one said.

'Anyone a medic?' Carter asked.

No one put their hand up.

'Can someone call it in?' Carter crouched down beside the guy. 'I'm trained in basic first aid.'

'Me too,' Willow told him.

'I never saw him coming. He shot right out in front of me on his skateboard.' A woman stood by the car that had knocked the guy down, her hands gripped in front of her. 'I didn't have time to stop.'

Willow awkwardly joined Carter, her muscles stiff from her strenuous workout in the water. Something sharp stabbed her good knee. 'Ow. Be careful. There're pieces of metal on the road.' What from was anyone's guess.

'Could be off the skateboard,' a woman standing next to her said and held up a bent wheel frame. 'Seems to be missing nuts and bolts.'

'That'd do it.' Willow turned her concentration to the man lying between her and Carter. 'Hello? Can you hear me?'

'What happened?' he croaked, opening and closing his eyes rapidly.

'You were hit by a car. Don't move. We'll check you over,' she told him. One leg was twisted under his backside at an odd angle. A large gash tore through his cheek. There'd be more to come, Willow was sure. Hopefully help would get here fast.

Carter was checking the leg that looked broken. 'I'm not moving this. The paramedics can sort it.'

Willow reached for the man's wrist, felt for his pulse. 'Erratic.'

'Slightly raised, nothing to worry about now,' she noted after sixty seconds, glad she'd kept up regular first-aid training. She'd started when she began competitive road cycling as there were often accidents and someone needing help.

'That's probably shock induced,' Carter assured her. 'Can't be too different from our patients.'

'Stay still,' she reiterated as the man tried to sit up. Was spinal damage likely?

'What happened?' he demanded again through a bubble of blood, seeming oblivious to his surroundings.

'Ambulance is on its way,' someone called.

Carter glanced at her briefly. 'Hold his shoulders down so he can't try lifting himself up. He shouldn't be moving his head either.'

'He's very agitated.'

'I think that's due to shock too. I can't smell alcohol.' Carter held the guy's chin and opened his mouth, peered in. 'Wish I had a glove in my back pocket. There are broken teeth with fragments in his mouth. Don't want him swallowing those.' He scooped a finger around the man's mouth, flicked a tooth fragment out.

Willow kept a tight hold on the man's shoulders as he tried to roll away from Carter.

A tooth was flicked out. 'There, think I've got everything.' Carter pulled back.

'Here.' A woman handed him a packet of antiseptic wipes.

'Thanks.'

'What about the left arm?' Willow said. 'It's at an odd angle. Think we should move it?'

'Best leave it to the paramedics. They'll have the gear on hand in case movement causes serious bleeding from a wound we haven't seen.'

'Let me go,' the guy cried. 'You're hurting me.'

'Steady, mate,' Carter told him. 'You need to stay still to prevent hurting yourself any more. Willow's trying to help you. She knows what she's doing. Trust her, okay?'

Blimey. Where'd that come from? Concentrating on examining the lacerations before her, she tried to ignore the glow of warmth Carter's words brought. This wasn't quite the same as when she'd saved Axel.

Axel. She glanced across to the gate leading into the vet clinic's yard, hoping the pup was all right being left alone so abruptly. At least he couldn't go anywhere. The fence was high and she had closed the gate.

'Seems you took the brunt of the impact on your left side,' Carter told the man.

'He hit the front of the car,' the woman who'd been driving said in a quavering voice somewhere behind Willow. 'He came out of nowhere right into my path.'

Sirens were coming closer. Willow felt some of the tension slip away. This guy would have the help he needed in a few minutes. As for the driver who'd struck him, she had no answers. The truck driver that had crashed into the group of cyclists she had been with had said much the same thing, only to be proven to have been speeding with alcohol in his system. He was boarding with the government at the moment.

'What's your name, mate?' Carter was busy trying to distract the guy now groaning deeply. He didn't get an answer. Hopefully that didn't mean he was losing consciousness. 'Mate? What's your name?'

'What've we got?' A paramedic knelt down beside Willow.

'Seems this man was skateboarding when he crossed the road directly into the path of an oncoming car. All the impact appears to be on the left side. He's in shock, has been aware we're here, but now seems to have lost concentration. We haven't been able to get any information from him.'

Carter rattled off the scant injury details they had, and told the paramedic, 'I removed tooth fragments from his mouth. He's also bitten his tongue.'

'You know what you're doing,' the paramedic said. 'Nurse or doctor?'

'Vet. And vet nurse.' He nodded at Willow.

The paramedic grinned. 'Guess the guy got lucky.'

Willow drew a breath and stood up, rubbing her thigh where it ached.

Carter was watching her.

Her hand stilled. Then started moving up and down again. To hell with it. Having a prosthesis came with aches on bad days. 'Good luck,' she said to the guy on the ground, doubting he heard her. She just had to put it out there. Who knew what lay ahead for him?

As they stepped through the gate into the clinic's yard, Carter looked at her with something like admiration. 'You're good. Calm and confident.'

'I try to be.' She studied him. He really was something else. Absolutely drop-dead gorgeous in ways that were becoming more obvious the longer she was around him. 'You knew what you were doing too.'

'Guess the boundaries between human and animal injuries aren't too far apart in some instances.' A knee-knocking smile was expanding as he watched her. 'We make a good team, don't we?'

'Not bad at all.' Her breathing was a little hitched, as if her lungs weren't sure if they should be inhaling or exhaling.

'Sit down at the table and I'll get some antiseptic to clean that cut on your leg.'

'What?' Glancing down, she shook her head at the sight of blood oozing down her shin. 'I forgot all about that.' It wasn't a big deal, more a small scratch. 'I'll be fine.'

'You're around a dog. Best cover the cut with a plaster.'

'Fair enough.' Sinking onto a seat by the table, she rubbed her other thigh until Axel approached and placed his head by her hand. 'You want a pat?'

His head pressed harder against her.

'That's a yes, then.'

'Right.' Carter appeared before her and knelt down. 'Stretch your leg out for me.' He wore vinyl gloves.

'I can do it.'

Stern eyes met her gaze. 'I'm sure you can.'

Okay, she couldn't argue with that look. When this man meant business it seemed there was no holding back. Pushing her leg forward, she went back to patting Axel. His hard head was warm to her touch. Even warmer were the strong strokes of cotton on her knee and down her shin. Firm, methodical, and making her blink as though from a deep sleep.

'That's quite a deep cut,' her vet said.

'I landed heavily.' Clumsy really, but she'd been focused on the man lying on the road. 'You're not about to sew me back together, are you?' The sooner he stopped wiping those cotton wipes over her skin, the sooner she would breathe properly again. A bit of stitching might calm her suddenly racing heart. It was all a bit OTT considering she didn't get wound up over men. Except Carter seemed to be doing things to her she hadn't experienced in a long time.

Ignore him.

Was it as easy as that? When she ached to reach out and touch him?

'I'll put a butterfly plaster on to keep the edges together. It's nothing serious.' His voice was low and controlled, as though he was having trouble focusing too.

Holding out her hand, she said, 'Let me do that.'

He shook his head abruptly. 'Stop moving your leg.' He was patting her skin dry with a tissue, his focus entirely on the small abrasion causing all the trouble.

Best she did as she was told and get this over sooner. Because, odd as it sounded, having Carter touching her leg was a turn-on.

Moments later Carter stood up. 'There you go.'

'Thanks. Now I've been treated by a vet.' A wide smile suddenly broke across her mouth. 'There's a first.'

He was watching her as he pulled the gloves off. 'Hope I was as gentle as a doctor.'

'Far more.' Her experience of doctors didn't include making her heat up on the inside and want to touch them. She stood up abruptly. Axel jumped back. Carter didn't move. 'You're good. I'm impressed.'

Not saying I'd like more of your touch on my skin—without the gloves.

'You're easily impressed.' His lips were soft and enthralling.

'Wrong. I'm fussy.' Taking a step closer, she enjoyed the sight before her. He fascinated her with his intense good looks and how quickly he awakened her dormant desires.

Carter came nearer, his hands taking her upper arms gently. His gaze was intense and unwavering. 'How fussy?'

'For me to know.' Her head felt light as her body responded to his intensity. And those mesmerising lips.

'And me to find out.' Carter's lips touched hers softly, as if asking permission to kiss her.

Willow pressed forward, opening her mouth under his. Slid her arms around his waist. Held him against her. Held herself against his firm, solid body. And kissed him. All because he'd been looking after her leg.

Try again, Willow. Try because he is attractive and exciting.

Okay, fine.

He kissed her back. Again, and again.

Then she knew nothing but them and the hot sensations tripping throughout her. Felt nothing but Carter's heat and his lips on hers, his tongue in her mouth.

Thump. Axel head-butted her good leg.

'Hey.' A timely reminder that she didn't usually do kissing a man she barely knew. Or any man. She flipped her head back and gazed at Carter. Especially one she was about to work for.

He was looking down at her, a broad smile on those luscious lips, and a twinkle in his eyes. 'Definitely a good team.'

'True.' She hadn't known kisses like Carter's. Not for a long time, any rate. Which was scary, because he'd made her forget everything else. Even to breathe. Getting intense with men wasn't safe. She might lose her heart and then she'd be forever worrying she might lose the man she gave it to. There was no way she could again go through the pain and grief she'd known when her friends died. She didn't have it in her. Her life had been destroyed last time. The sense of belonging with friends and family, of being comfortable in her own skin, had gone, replaced with an undeniable loneliness and longing for what wasn't to be.

'Willow? You all right?'

'Yes.' Not really, but now wasn't the time to be talking about her past. Or how it rattled her. No, Carter had done the rattling. 'I'd better be getting home. I'm on dinner tonight.' As if her flatmates would be sitting around waiting for her to turn up.

'Come on, then. We'll put Axel to bed, and you can head away.' He didn't look relieved or annoyed. Maybe she hadn't stirred him with her kisses half as much as he had her.

She was out of practice, but she'd swear she'd put everything she had into kissing him. It had come naturally. He'd made her feel so special and needed, and she'd lost control of her usual restraints. 'Whatever you think.' She hoped that didn't mean this was normal for Carter, that he had no boundaries when it came to getting pleasure from women. Had she just made the biggest fool of herself ever?

Carter took her hand and tugged her to a stop. 'I think—no, I know I'm glad you dropped by tonight. Might've been to see Axel, but it was me you kissed.' There was a wicked glint in those beautiful eyes that cut straight through her reticence. Then he jerked back, dropping her hand. 'Sorry, I've behaved badly. You're an employee as of tomorrow. I shouldn't have kissed you.' He ran a hand through his hair. 'It's wrong.'

Where did that leave her? Being honest, as always. 'It doesn't have to be. I'm only here for eight weeks, filling in while your nurse is on leave. This doesn't have to jeopardise the day-to-day workings of the clinic. *And* we're both adults.'

'Of that I have no doubt.' He put more distance between them.

She got it in spades. He didn't want to take this any further. She'd have to find someone else to ask to partner her to the wedding, or go alone and ignore the I-told-you-so look in Dave's eyes. 'I'll put Axel away and head home.'

'Willow, wait.' Again his fingers slid through his hair. 'About partnering you to the wedding.'

'Forget I asked. I understand it means stepping over the boss-employee boundaries.' They were a vet and a vet nurse going about caring for animals, but surely it couldn't hurt to spend a day together. If he thought that was wrong, then so be it. She'd survive the empty chair beside her at the wedding. And do her damnedest to forget those kisses.

'What date?'

'Saturday fortnight. Nearly three weeks.'

'Count me in.'

What?

'I like challenges.' His smile was slow in coming, but when it arrived her head spun.

'Are you sure?'

'You want someone to support you. I get it. Though I'd have preferred you invited me because you enjoyed my company.' He was still smiling but there was some longing in his expression she wasn't quite understanding.

She needed to be honest, but this was awkward. 'I know it sounded as if I was desperate and would've asked just about any male my age or older, but that's not quite true. I liked you from the moment we met last night, and I feel comfortable with you.' She was not going to be so honest as to say, 'I got hot and wound up.' 'I'm glad you're coming with me.'

CHAPTER THREE

IT MIGHT BE a few weeks away, but he needed to go through his wardrobe and check out what he had to wear to the wedding, Carter thought as he laid the corgi he'd just spayed inside her designated cage. There were some classy shirts he hadn't worn yet, and two pairs of smart trousers, but he might hit the shops anyway. He couldn't be too casual when he was taking Willow on a date.

He laughed at himself. Who was he kidding? He loved dressing up all smart and stylishly and didn't do it often enough. *And* he really wanted to impress Willow. That was a first in a long time. Something that should have him on edge. Becoming interested in a stunning woman could only lead to heartache. Yet for the first time ever he felt willing to take a chance. That was unless he'd misread Willow entirely and she was selfish and controlling. He couldn't see that being the case. She was strong, mentally and physically, but didn't appear to expect everyone else to jump when she said so.

Her strength was obvious from how she'd lifted Axel into her car the other day, when it must've hurt her stump, and brought him here for help. How she'd dropped to her knees to aid the guy who'd been struck by a car, not a thought for her own discomfort as she hunkered down on the tarmac. And how she got on with checking out the animals brought in here or overnighting after some trauma.

He was *not* thinking how the woman could kiss like there was no tomorrow. Hell, no. Except that was a lie. It was *all* he'd been thinking about ever since she'd walked out of his arms and out of the clinic on Tuesday, only to return dressed in scrubs this morning, nothing but a quiet smile for him as everyone sat down in the tearoom and introduced themselves to Willow. He wanted more of those kisses. They filled him with energy. The world was brighter.

'You're bouncing around a lot this morning.' Kathy, receptionist and accounts manager, and Seamus' partner, laughed as he placed a file on her desk. 'Like you've got ants in your pants.'

'There was a nest out the back of my house

but I thought I'd dealt with it,' he retorted around a grin. Had he really become such a dull creature? His brothers often told him he needed to get a life, but had he withdrawn so much everyone thought he was a sad puppy?

'Your next patient is ready,' Willow called from the operating room in a normal, let's-get-on-with-it voice.

He couldn't help wondering though—how did she feel about their kiss? She didn't appear uncomfortable with him; nor was she looking as if she wanted to leap up against him and press that beautiful mouth against his again.

I've news for you. Willow, I want to kiss you again.

That was so against anything he'd felt for a woman in a long time, it scared the pants off him.

'Carter?'

He jumped. 'Coming.'

'More bouncing happening,' Kathy chortled.

Tootsy needed part of her back paw amputated after getting caught in a trap. Tootsy was very much a hunting cat so her owner didn't think this operation would hold her back from getting out into more trouble for very long. Nothing appeared to hold Willow back either. Funny how every subject around here brought him back to Willow. He hardly knew her, but he wanted to spend more time with her outside the clinic. Not starting with the wedding. That was ages away. No, they had to get together much sooner or he'd implode with frustration.

'Tootsy's sedated,' Willow reminded him. She must think he wasn't very professional.

Willow was an enigma. He wanted to know so much about her, and yet did he really want to find out all that made her tick? That meant getting involved on a level he didn't do, and hadn't since Cassandra. It was all very well enjoying the lightness in his chest in the two days since he'd met her, but where would it lead? It might be time to step outside the barriers he'd erected around himself, but whether Willow was the right woman to be taking that chance with was a conundrum that he wasn't ready for. Still, he couldn't let go the feeling she might be what he needed.

Carter snapped on gloves and picked up a syringe. 'Right, Toots, let's get you sorted.'

Willow was petting the cat. 'You'll be able to run around on the stump, Tootsy.'

'Give her a few weeks and I reckon she'll be back hunting. It'll be tender at first but eventually she'll be used to it and I suspect

there'll be no stopping her from hunting
again.'

Willow handed him the scalpel. 'Here we
go, Tootsy.' She ran a hand over the soft black
and white fur on the cat's shoulder. 'You'll
feel so much better without that smashed foot
to drag around.'

The cat had been caught in a pest trap in
the barn on the farm where she lived, and had
dragged herself two hundred metres to the
farmhouse with the trap attached. 'A toughie,
isn't she?'

'That'll bode well for getting used to being
short of some of her paw.' Willow swabbed
the area he was incising, her fingers deft and
gentle. Not once did she wince as he removed
the mangled paw piece.

When he sutured, she swabbed, passed
him a new, threaded needle the moment he'd
finished with the one in hand. The perfect
nurse.

As soon as the op was finished, Willow
was back in his thoughts in other ways. She
seemed very aware of everything he did during the short surgery. As if she kept an eye
on anything and everything she was involved
in, keeping ahead of trouble. By the sound of
it, she'd been a cyclist. 'Were you a competitive cyclist?' If so she'd have been alert for

other cyclists, the road conditions, how far she'd travelled and still had to go.

'Yes. My field was long-distance racing.' She was settling Tootsy in a cage, making sure no weight was placed on the surgical site.

'Only in Australia?'

'And offshore.' She wasn't very forthcoming.

Fair enough. They'd finished for the morning. Surgeries done. Seamus was doing the appointment list. Joe was out on the rural rounds. 'Time for some coffee and a sandwich,' he said.

'Bring it on.' Her laugh was low and sexy. He was probably making that up, but who cared? It made him feel good. 'I'll be there as soon as I've cleaned up,' she told him.

Kathy was in the kitchen downing a salad. 'How's it going?'

Meaning how's the new nurse working out? 'Good. All the surgeries went well.'

'So Willow knows what she's doing.' Kathy grinned. 'Does she understand she's got you in a pickle?'

Was it that obvious? It must be, yet he'd have sworn he managed to keep a straight face around Willow, at least when other staff were about. 'Hope not,' he muttered and got another laugh in reply.

'You're too easy to read, Carter. Better practise your game face if you don't want everyone giving you a hard time.' Kathy rinsed her plate and mug, put them in the dishwasher. 'Need anything from the supermarket? I'm heading down there now.'

'Can't think of anything, thanks. Unless you think I should wear a mask?' He laughed, something that came more readily than ever these past couple of days.

'I'll see if there's one that'll match your shirt,' she said as she headed out of the door.

'What's Kathy looking for to match your shirt?' Willow asked a moment later as she entered, opening her pack of sandwiches as though she were dying of hunger.

'A tie?'

An eloquent eye roll was directed at him. 'Something for an exuberant puppy to bite?'

'Makes their visit fun.' He waved a mug at her. 'Coffee?'

Her brows came together as she stared at him. Finally she said, 'Sounds good,' and bit into a sandwich.

When he'd made their coffees he sat opposite her at the table. 'You finding everything all right?'

'No problems whatsoever. The set-up's consistent with most veterinary clinics I've worked in. Almost like vets sit a paper on the subject.'

'More often than not, clinics are tight on space so there's not a lot of choice over where everything goes. While this one is larger than normal, we've kept to the routine. Don't alter what works.'

'I'll take Axel for a short walk to stretch that leg when I've finished my lunch.'

'I've put some things together you might need for him while he's at your house.' She'd finally agreed to take the pup home every night until Mrs Burnside was discharged from hospital. He got the feeling Willow adored looking after Axel but might be worried over giving him up in a few days.

'I saw the pile by the back entrance. You didn't need to provide food for him. I was going to get that on the way home.'

'Our contribution to helping him.' Before he could overthink it he asked, 'I was wondering if you'd like to go for a beer after we close? Tonight?'

Silence met him. She took a mouthful of coffee, staring at the tabletop. It seemed she never made spontaneous decisions. He waited.

Finally she looked up. 'I'd like that. Where?'

Phew. At least that was what he thought he felt. This was alien territory for him, and while it was exciting it was also worrying. He might be starting something he wouldn't be able to stop. 'Turf and Surf suit you?' He didn't know where she lived. 'Or is there another place you'd prefer?'

'Turf and Surf's good. I can walk there from home.'

'I could pick you up.'

'Thanks, but I like to stretch my legs after a day on my feet. Gets rid of the aches.' There was a deep weariness in her voice that suggested her prosthesis ground her down at times. That was no surprise. It must've been a huge shock to lose her lower leg, a trauma that would affect her for ever.

'Fine.' He wouldn't persist with his offer. She might change her mind about meeting up altogether. That would not be good. This was an opportunity to test the relationship waters with. Unsure if it was time to step up and let go of the past, he was becoming more convinced it was time to try.

Then Willow gasped. 'I can't do that. What about Axel? I can't leave him at home alone on his first night.'

'Bring him with you. They have an area

outside at the pub where patrons can have their dogs with them.'

'Done.' She screwed up the paper bag her sandwich had been in and tossed it at the bin. 'I'll go and see how he is.' Picking up her coffee, she headed away.

Leaving Carter disappointed. Even the mundane became interesting when Willow was around. As he stirred his coffee he couldn't let go of the sound of her voice. She was going out with him after work, so she must be a little bit interested in him. He smiled. How good was that? It felt like an opportunity to move forward, to start living again, as his brothers kept nagging him about. Was there a chance they might have a short fling? Did he want to? If it opened up possibilities for the future then yes, he was all for it. And if it didn't? Then he could say he'd tried. Willow might think he was crazy but there was no harm in thinking about it.

What had happened to her? Had she been dealt a blow so huge it had cut her down big time? Losing her leg would've been traumatic whatever the circumstances, but he sensed there was more to it. She'd said she was with other cyclists when it happened. She mightn't have been the only person to be injured. Cyclists rode in groups, using each other for smooth air. A truck wasn't a small vehicle and could make a huge impact.

The need to know more about Willow was getting to him. He picked up his phone. Where had the accident occurred? Willow came from Sydney. He'd start there. Tap, tap on the screen. He shouldn't be doing this. It felt too personal. Better to ask her outright. But what if she didn't like that? She might react by walking away from him.

Close the screen. Leave it for Willow to tell you if she wants to.

Easy to say. He wanted to know more about this woman playing with his mind. That permanent weariness in the depth of her eyes drew him in, made him yearn to hug it all away for her. But until he had some idea of what caused the weariness he couldn't help her.

Deep breath. He'd tell her what he was doing when the right time arose. Tap. Type: *Sydney, truck versus cyclists accident.*

Four years ago, she'd said.

Tap.

The screen filled with a list of headlines, all about a truck and trailer unit that crashed into a group of cyclists on the Sydney harbour bridge. Carter's finger shook as he opened the first article. A picture of a large freight truck on its side with the trailer on two wheels and cyclists and their bikes thrown in all directions. The headline read *Two Dead. Three Seriously Injured.*

He sat back, his heart thudding. The scene was horrendous. How anyone survived was beyond him. Willow was lucky not to have lost more than her lower leg.

But she had. There were those two who died. She'd have known them. Maybe very well. Even if they hadn't been best friends, it would've been appalling dealing with the outcomes of that day. No wonder that weariness was ever-present. If he was reading her right, and he thought he might be. Quickly perusing the article, he clicked on to another, but it had nothing more to add. Further down a headline read: *Driver in Court on Charge of Dangerous Driving.*

Tom Edwards had pleaded guilty to driving well over the speed limit when he had lost control of the truck, which had then jackknifed into two cars and a group of five cyclists on a training ride for the national coastal race. Edwards had also pleaded not guilty to two charges of homicidal driving. The trial was set to last three days.

Next headline: *Edwards Guilty of Homicidal Driving.*

Carter closed the site. He'd seen enough. He didn't need more details to know Willow had been dealt a massive blow. He'd already come to the conclusion she was a strong woman, a fighter with a soft heart. There was no denying the way her eyes had filled with love as she'd petted Axel. Did she do that for her human friends? There'd been no mention of a boyfriend, and she'd asked him to go to the wedding with her, so she must be single. Although there could be a guy back in Sydney or some other place she'd worked.

The coffee was hot on his tongue. He put the mug aside. This was about his own trust issues coming to the fore. He quashed them. Since he and Cassandra had grown up together, had known all there was to know about each other, he'd thought no other woman could get to him like this. That wasn't quite right. He hadn't believed Cass could do what she did either. She'd cut him off at the knees on their supposed wedding day.

So the fact he thought about Willow well into the night after going to bed underlined how interested he was. Add in how his body heated every time he saw her and he was fast becoming a lost cause.

Carter sighed. He was good at fooling himself. At least he usually was. It didn't seem to be working right now though. His smile felt rueful. Nothing was easy. Until Willow, the handbrake had always been firmly in place. Could he be in need of some fun and excitement before he got back on track, keeping his life compartmentalised?

'Carter, I'm sorry if I sounded reluctant about tonight. I am looking forward to it.' Willow stood in the doorway, looking worried.

Knock him down, why didn't she? Unprecedented relief poured through him. 'Glad to hear it. But I was going with your "I'd like that" anyway while ignoring everything else.' That wasn't quite true, but he'd keep that to himself, and go with the happiness engulfing him. As long as he came out the other side without being hurt it would be worth the effort of keeping her cheerful.

'Cheers for that. I'll get the spaniel ready for his hernia op.'

'I'll be there shortly,' he replied to her back. Brilliant. They had a date. Denying the apprehensions that picked at him, he went with the happiness bubbling through him. Life was looking better by the hour. The sun hadn't just risen that morning; it had painted his world with light and warmth. Filled him with hope for a future that might hold some love and fulfilment of his dreams.

Willow twisted around so she could check out her backside in the shop window. The new jeans highlighted her shape and flattened the curves on her hips. 'Not too bad,' she muttered. Hopefully Carter was distracted from the odd shape of her knee. Not that he seemed too concerned about her prosthesis. It was kind of nice not having to talk about it, when it was usually the first thing guys asked about. Nothing about where she came from, or what she did for a living. Apparently that was boring compared to her accident.

There was nothing boring about Carter. He already had her fingers tingling and she still had to walk inside the pub and see him.

A light chuckle reached her from the other side of the road. 'Like what I see,' called Carter.

Heat soared in her cheeks. Caught. Idiot. Now he'd think she was into herself. These days she did have some issues about her looks. Who wouldn't in the circumstances? She might put it out there she didn't care about the scars and her leg, but deep down she did. When people stared, it hurt. She wanted to shout that she was a real person and had feelings like everyone else. Instead she kept quiet. There was nothing to be gained by making her feelings known. 'Just checking I haven't sat on anything messy before I left home.'

'I'm not even going there.' Carter joined her. 'I will say you scrub up well after a day with dogs and cats in any number of conditions. That shade of green matches the specks in your blue eyes, and the jeans fit perfectly.'

So he could be charming. She'd enjoy it, pretend it meant little while basking in the glow. How often did she get compliments about her body? Okay, so he was talking about her blouse and her jeans, but they were covering her body nicely. 'Say hello to Axel.'

Carter laughed. 'Hello, Axel.' Then he looked back to her. 'You know what? It was one of the best days I've had at the clinic in a while.'

What was he saying? 'Because there were no major traumas?'

He nodded lightly. 'Routine surgeries, the usual distressed pets and more distressed owners. Not saying I enjoy that side of my work. I hate seeing people upset about their fur babies. No, I enjoyed being there more than usual. Nothing I can put my finger on.

It was as if a weight had been lifted off my shoulders that I didn't know I had.'

Quite a speech for this man. Not the abrupt two-word statements he had made that first time she met him with Axel in her arms. But he had been quite a bit more verbal since. 'That's great. We'll drink to more days like it.'

'Here's to hoping we don't get interrupted by someone needing medical attention. Or an animal.' Carter tapped his glass of beer against hers minutes later. 'We seem to attract accident victims.'

She tapped back. 'I don't know that it's too bad. We work well together even in different medical situations.' Carter was easy to work alongside. Not all vets were as accommodating of their nurses. She'd heard one or two say the nurses were there to take the bites from upset animals because they were more expendable than the vets. It was true up to a point, she supposed, but rather unpleasant.

'It's usually takes a little time for a new staff member to fit in, but you've slotted in so easily it's like you've always worked alongside me.'

'Same. It could be because I move around from clinic to clinic and have worked with numerous vets.' She'd been told often enough she was good at her job to believe it. Working with Carter was no different, other than that she liked his company more than most vets she'd known. Tomorrow she'd be working with Joe and, while that should go just as well, she wouldn't be feeling as soft towards him as Carter, who'd be doing the rural rounds.

'Your new friend looks happy enough.' He watched the pup doing a circle of the mat, trying to get comfortable.

'He seems fine. I rang Mrs Burnside when I got home to tell her where he was and how he was coping. When she's able to move around a bit, we're going to arrange it so she can be wheeled down to the entrance where I'll be waiting with Axel.'

'That would be awesome. It must be hard for her not having Axel there when she's obviously in a bad way and needing all the loving she can get.'

'I reckon,' Willow agreed. She had briefly thought of getting a dog again for the unconditional love pets gave out, but it would be selfish with all the moving around she did.

'You ever had a dog? Or a cat?' Carter was watching her in that thoughtful way of his.

'I once had a German Shepherd. Lizzy. She was adorable. It was really hard when she got old and had to go.'

'You said you moved around too much these days to have a pet. Is being nomadic a recent thing?' He spoke light-heartedly but there was a depth in his eyes that suggested it was a loaded question.

He wanted to know more about her past? Or was he just trying to get to know her? 'There are many places to see and I am no-where near ready to settle down. Plenty of years ahead for that.' If she got lucky and fate didn't step in as it had done for Dee and Jess.

'I'm moving on from here when my contract finishes.' It wasn't the first time she'd mentioned it, but reminding him meant he could never say she'd misled him into thinking she was available for more than a fling. 'I came to the Gold Coast in the first place because of my friend's wedding, getting the last job for five months. Unfortunately that left me with a couple more months to fill in so when Joe contacted my boss up there to ask if he knew of any nurses wanting temporary work I jumped at the opportunity.'

'So you aren't interested in taking up another contract on the Gold Coast or even up in Brisbane when your time's up with us? I know you want to see other places but what's wrong with visiting them during vacation breaks? Why live offshore?'

Of course he didn't understand. He didn't know that she'd lost her friends when they were in their prime and that they'd missed out on so much she was afraid of missing too. The odds of something as terrible happening to her again were remote, but that didn't mean it wouldn't happen. 'It's what I do. I'm not ready to stop, and might never be. There's a huge world out there to discover.'

Be forewarned, Carter. Don't expect anything more from me than here and now. There's no point in getting close to me. I'll only let you down.

It was good she was only here for two months. There was less to lose if they got further involved.

'I appreciate your honesty,' he said.

But did he understand it? Doubtful. He had no idea what caused her restlessness.

'Just saying.' Because she was restless. No doubt about it. Stopping in one place, creating a home for herself, making lasting friends, starting a relationship with a wonderful man were the things her dreams were made of. Dreams she didn't dare follow up on. Dreams could disappear in a blink. Mostly it didn't bother her. She knew how to hide her concerns from herself. They were buried so deep it took a lot to bring them to the surface. So why could she suddenly see them now? Had Carter got to her that much already she could no longer deny them? He'd better not have. She so wasn't ready to take any risk with her heart, or anything else.

'I can't imagine not having my two dogs. They both came from the rescue centre at different times. They're getting on in years so are more than happy lying around the yard going nowhere. Though a walk on the beach is always accepted with lots of wags.'

A picture of Carter striding along the beach, two dogs bounding along beside him, filled her mind, and a rare envy enveloped her. He had the settled life she only thought of as a dream, not for real. A home in town, pets and, as far as she'd ascertained, a steady career. It sounded like bliss. 'Why are you practising in town when you're a country boy at heart?'

'The clinic does quite a lot of rural work and that side is growing. I do prefer domestic animals. It is quite different working with a cattle beast. They're not as accommodating when I'm poking and prodding their bodies.' He was certainly opening up to her, with a soft smile thrown in. 'As for the rural life-style, my brothers are farmers and my parents are still on the land. I help out when needed.'

She could get used to this. Best not. Two months and she'd be gone. 'Keep that foremost in your mind, Willow,' sounded the voice of wisdom in the back of her head. Ignoring it, she asked, 'You haven't found anyone special to share your life with?'

'No.'

Right. Stay away from that subject. Fair enough. It was personal, and he probably wasn't ready to talk quite that much about himself. Just as she wasn't. 'Sorry. Ignore that. I can be a bit intense at times.' What next? Their glasses were empty. 'Want another beer?'

He was on his feet before she'd finished asking. 'I'll get them. Would you like to have dinner here?'

Eager to move on from her blunder, she said, 'You bet.'

'I'll grab a couple of menus.'

He didn't need to. She already knew what she wanted. This had become her go-to place when she or her flatmates couldn't be bothered cooking dinner. She hadn't seen Carter here before, and he would be hard to miss. That tall, fit body, the thick mop of blond hair, those sensuous eyes that said, *Look at me*. Carter wasn't an ego. He wasn't demanding to be noticed, but it was impossible not to watch him.

She glanced around, saw she wasn't the only female in the room eying him up. *Forget it, ladies. He's mine.* For the next hour or two anyway. Then, who knew? She'd leave that up to time and whatever unravelled. Which was unlike her. Being definite and focused about herself was the only way to cope. Then along came Carter and all her practised moves flew out of the window. There could be something in that she was missing. But he wasn't going to be hers long term.

'Here you go.' Carter slid a glass and the menu in her direction.

'Cheers.' Pushing the menu aside, she said, 'I'll have the salt and pepper squid when we're ready.'

'You've been here before.' He grinned.

'Once or twice. I lived down here while working in Brisbane.'

He looked thoughtful as he took a mouthful of beer. 'To answer your question more fully, I've been single for five years.'

She hadn't expected to be told that. 'A long time.'

'Yes and no. Sometimes it feels that way, other times I'm quite happy plodding along in my life. I have a close-knit family for the days it gets too lonely, which isn't very often,' he added in a hurry.

'I wasn't thinking you were a sad sack feeling sorry for yourself.'

His smile was gentle. 'Just making sure you understood.' He took another mouthful. 'I was engaged to my childhood sweetheart, but she called it off at the very last minute.'

Willow reached for his free hand and held it for a moment. 'I can't begin to imagine what that was like. *Is* like. She must've been crazy. You're a great guy.'

Too much, Willow, however true it is.

He was wonderful, and she didn't know much about him. Yet. He'd been hurt, badly. It was there in his suddenly sad voice, in the depth of his gaze. He was wary of starting again. Welcome to her world. Different reasons but they both had trust issues. Another reason to tread carefully.

Turning his hand over, Carter gave hers a squeeze. 'Thank you.'

She smiled, feeling comfortable, even happy despite his hurt. 'Tell me more about your family. I've got a brother in Sydney, who's a criminal lawyer and enjoys being single. My parents are usually supportive of everything we do, and are always there when I need a shoulder to bawl on.'

'You wouldn't think of returning to Sydney?'

No, there were too many memories she didn't want to face. 'Not yet, if at all.' That was the most he was getting on that particular subject.

'Fair enough.'

He accepted her answer so easily? But then, she had told him she wasn't ready to settle down at all. 'We're opposites, you and I. You live in the region you grew up in. I keep moving around, not even contemplating returning home.' Right, time to lighten up the mood. She could only give out so much info about herself, and she'd already gone beyond the line. 'I like it that way.'

'I trained to become a vet here in Queensland, and then went into practice with two friends. There haven't been reasons to head away long term. I've no desire to leave behind all I know. I'm okay with where I'm at.' Surprise flitted through his eyes, gone in a flash.

He hadn't realised that? So much for moving on to something light and entertaining. 'What are you having for dinner?'

Getting desperate, Willow.

Carter suddenly laughed. 'Same as you. But there's no hurry. Unless you want to get home soon?'

'Nope. I'm happy here.' *With you.*

Snap. They were on the same page. Hanging out with Willow over an easy meal and a couple of beers was a great way to finish the day. With Axel as a chaperone. Not that he had any intention of getting too close. Too soon, and caution was rife in his head. Except they had kissed last night. It would be kind of hard to turn away from a repeat kiss if it was on offer. He didn't even want to.

'Are you sure it's all right to be out together when you're one of my bosses?' she interrupted his thoughts.

'I can't see anything wrong. Anyway, I mentioned to Joe we were going for a drink and a meal and he was more than happy.' More like he was cheeky, suggesting it might be an opportunity for Carter to find someone to remind him of what he was missing out on and have a bloody good time while he was at it. Also a permanent replacement for the nurse on leave who looked as if she might not return wouldn't go astray. Friends. Who needed them? If Joe hadn't said it first,

Seamus would've found an opportunity. He grinned. 'Hope you don't mind.'

She didn't look at all concerned. 'Best to keep things out in the open.'

Not everything, he thought. Their kisses weren't for sharing. 'Glad you see it that way.' He stood up. 'I'll order the food.' He needed to take a break out of her space.

'I can get the meals.' A fiery independence came into her eyes.

'Willow, I asked you to join me. It's my treat.' Hopefully there'd be other nights like this. Could be Joe knew him better than he knew himself, because he was enjoying time with Willow, finding plain old fun spending a few hours socialising with a lovely woman did have a way of getting under his skin.

'Thank you,' she said. 'I feel awkward about you paying, that's all.'

'Why?'

'Let's just say I haven't been treated quite as well as I used to be by men since I lost my leg.' She was watching him closely.

Was she looking for a grimace? Thinking he might flinch at the reminder of her disability? *Think again, Willow.* 'Don't judge us all by the same standard. I for one can see beyond the picture you present to the world.' Damn it, he'd just put out more than he intended. She didn't need to know he was interested enough to look behind the tough façade she presented most of the time. 'I'm sure others can too if you give them a chance.' Now he was giving her a lecture. His hand found hers, covered it. 'I think I understand your need to be strong, but don't let that take over when something good's on offer.'

Her head jerked back, and she stared at him, but her hand remained in his. He took that as a good sign.

'Carter,' she croaked. Swallowing, she started again. 'Carter, I'm sorry if you think I was having a crack at you. I was merely trying to explain where I was coming from. I hadn't realised you'd already figured it out.' Another swallow followed. 'Maybe I should've. You're one smart guy.'

'On that note, I'll go order our meals.' There was such a thing as saying too much. It tended to undo all the good already achieved.

Her smile was wonky, but appeared genuine. It certainly grabbed at his heart. Something he should be running from. But he didn't want to. He'd possibly reached the point in his life when he could put the past to bed. Willow ticked boxes he hadn't been aware of needing to fill in. It was almost as though he'd been waiting for someone like her to turn him around. Or was it just time? Did it really matter why so long as he didn't get hurt?

She's not staying on after her contract's up.

So he could get hurt. Or he could remain immune to those rare smiles and toe-tingling kisses, and have some fun. He was usually an all-in or all-out kind of guy. After Cass there hadn't been any inclination for all in, and he'd learned he wasn't a 'take her or leave her' kind of man when it came to women. They were as vulnerable as he could be, and he never wanted to be the one to break their heart.

'Same again?' the barmaid asked.

'Yes, and some food to go with it.'

'That'd be salt and pepper squid for one.' She laughed.

'For two.' He grinned. Another thing he shared with Willow. This was fun. But she deserved more than a casual fling. She didn't do risking her heart either. Whether because she'd lost her friends in that accident, or because some guy had broken her heart, he didn't know, but it was obvious in her caution, her toughness, and the softness that she tried to hide. Which might be a reason for her wanting a fling and nothing more involved. Much the same as him.

He knew that meant opening up and exposing his uncertainties. Learning to trust again. Something he firmly believed could never happen. If Cass could pull the plug on their relationship when they had known each other so well, when she had loved him as if they were joined at the hip, had understood him insanely well, then what chance did he have of finding someone else who'd fall for him and love him for ever? He wasn't prepared to give it a go. The years ahead looked bleak when he put it like that. No wife. No children. Being the single uncle, spoiling the nieces and nephews, was one thing. Having a tribe of his own was the next level up. *No. Cut it out. Get back in your hole.*

'Here're your drinks.' The barmaid placed their glasses on the mat.

'Thanks.'

Back at their table, he sat and stretched his legs to the side. Whatever was going on in his head, he was having fun like he hadn't known in ages. Tapping his glass to hers, he smiled. 'Cheers to us.'

'Cheers.' As easy as that.

Carter walked Willow back to the house she was staying at, taking it slowly as Axel limped along on the lead he held firmly in one hand. In the other hand was Willow's soft, warm one, her fingers interlaced with his. She seemed to be limping more than usual too. 'Tired?'

'Not really. I'm often sore by the end of the day. It's part of the deal. I'm used to it.' Her words were clipped, not inviting any further comment.

At least her hand remained in his. 'Are you enjoying working with us?' It sounded as if he was looking for a compliment since she'd been rostered with him. 'Do we operate the clinic similarly to others you've been at? Or is there room for improvement?'

'You're asking that of a nurse?' She puffed out a tight laugh.

'Why not? You might notice areas that could do with changes or sorting out that we've become used to and don't really see.' Didn't she think her career merited being noticed? 'You were very competent in all aspects of your work today. Therefore we'd listen to anything you might have to say.'

'That's a first.' Willow looked up at him, and stumbled.

'Easy.' Dropping her hand, he caught her arm, held her till she regained her balance and unwillingly let go. She mightn't appreciate him holding her arm as they walked, might see it as him thinking she needed help.

Already he understood Willow didn't take kindly to being treated as an invalid. She didn't come close. Everyone took tumbles; only she mightn't see it that way.

'Thanks.' Her hands shoved into the pockets of her trousers and she went for sauntering, as if she was saying, 'I'm fine. Don't underestimate me.'

Fair enough. Who was he to want to be there for her when she'd managed so well already? So he should forget her past injuries, concentrate on the current situation. He needed to kiss her. To hold that gorgeous body against him, and kiss her until her knees folded and she had to cling to him. Then kiss her some more. 'Willow.' He paused under a streetlight, and reached for her, looked into those all-seeing eyes. Yes, she'd known in an instant what he wanted because he couldn't hide the longing.

The tip of her tongue wet the centre of her top lip. 'Carter?'

She had to ask? He leaned in, placed his mouth over hers, and went with his feelings. She felt soft and yet demanding as she pressed her lips firmly against his. She tasted sexy as his tongue invaded her mouth. His body melted against hers as she stretched up against him, her arms around his waist holding tight. He couldn't get enough of her. They were kissing again. It was all he was aware of. Willow. Their joined mouths, their hot bodies pulsing against each other.

Thump. Something banged his knee.

Axel. The pup sat, pushed against his leg, staring up at him and Willow.

'Thanks, buddy. Wreck the fun, why don't you?'

Willow slipped out of his grasp and rubbed Axel's head. 'Spoilsport, aren't you?'

Taking her hand, at the same time tugging lightly on the lead, Carter set off down the road with that bounce back in his stride. They might have been interrupted, but Willow kissed like there was no tomorrow. She heated his blood like a match to straw, sending need spiralling throughout his body. He definitely wanted to follow through and make love. To forget everything from the past and leap forward, grabbing the opportunity as it presented. Willow had made it plain long term wasn't on offer, that she wasn't changing her mind. So, a fling? Why not? It felt good to him. He should ask her.

'Here we are.' She stopped at a letterbox. 'This is where I'm staying.'

His heart sank. There were three cars parked on the lawn, one Willow's. Lights shone from most of the windows. Their time alone had finished. They weren't starting anything else tonight.

Which might be just as well, came the voice of reason in his skull. Too fast, too soon. Or he'd just lost one night to enjoy being with Willow. Leaning closer, he grazed a light kiss on her mouth. 'See you tomorrow.' Then he walked away, head high, legs stretching out, heart pounding, stomach knotted. With no idea what was going on, or what he was going to do about it.

CHAPTER FOUR

'WILLOW, CAN YOU prepare Lucy for surgery?' Carter asked from the desk where he was typing up notes on the cat he'd just seen.

'Removing the hind dewclaws?' Willow asked, more because she loved the sound of his sexy voice than because she wasn't up to play with the Saturday morning surgery schedule.

'Yes. One was partially torn off when she was running through a hedge.'

'So why take the other off?' That she didn't know.

'The owner requested it, saying Lucy spends a lot of time in the creek and could easily catch the second one.' Definitely sexy.

She hadn't stopped thinking about the way he had kissed her the other night, and how she'd wanted to toss her clothes aside and get right up close to him. So much for not keeping her distance. He'd touched so many nerves she'd even asked her flatmates to think again if they knew of a man she could take to the wedding so that she could put space between her and Carter outside work. The relief when neither of them came up with a replacement only underlined how vulnerable Carter made her. She wanted him. Which was freaking her out. There was no way he was going to be the reason she didn't move on once her time here was up.

'Willow, got a minute?' Seamus called from the exam room next door. 'I need you to hold these puppies while I give them vaccinations.'

'Go,' Carter said. 'I'll be a few minutes with these notes.'

For a Saturday this clinic was busier than some she'd worked in. 'What a bunch of cuties,' she said as she spied the seven wriggling bundles of brown fur Seamus needed help with. Her heart lurched. She'd love one. To be there to raise and train him or her, to love and walk and cuddle. The catch being those three words—to be there. She wouldn't.

'Aren't they?' Seamus agreed. 'Let's get this done.'

They were being vaccinated against distemper and parvovirus. The first of a series of inoculations to come. 'Come here, little one.' She picked up the first one, a female, and held her firmly while rubbing gently with her thumbs, at the same time trying to deny the feeling of need gripping her. It wasn't the first time she'd known the urge to get a pup after working with them, but this time the sense of longing was deeper. Similar to her yearning for more with Carter.

'Next.' Seamus was fast. He dropped the syringe in a bowl and picked up the next from the line he'd laid out.

She doubted the pup had felt more than a light touch of the needle. She placed her in the portable cage the puppies had come in and picked up another from the clinic's basket. 'Hello, wee boy.'

I am not taking on a pet. I would be a terrible owner, always on the go, never settling one place for more than six months at the most.

'Next.'

Within minutes she was out of there and going to get Lucy from her cage. 'Your turn, my girl.'

Not your girl.

Another tug at her heart. Damn, she was turning into a right old softie since starting here. Her fourth day and the idea of getting a pet was grinding down the barriers around her heart. As was a certain vet who towered over her in a way that made her feel secure, not intimidated. A man's man without having to show it all the time. An understanding, caring human being who gave a lot to his animal patients. A guy who seemed to understand her in ways no one had since she'd lost her two friends.

Carter walked into the operating room. 'All set?'

Lucy was on the table, looking up at her with trusting eyes.

'It's all right, Lucy, you're going to be fine. Carter's going to make you sleepy so you don't feel a thing, and I'll be here all the time.'

Carter laughed. 'You are such a softie. Which is a good thing,' he added in a hurry. Worried she'd think he was having a poke at her?

'No softer than Lucy's vet, I'd say.'

'The downside to being a vet. Their big eyes filled with trust when they haven't a clue what's going on gets me every time.' He wasn't concerned about putting his feelings out there. Something else to like about him.

'Know what you mean.' That trust made her want to help the next animal that turned up, and the next.

As Carter injected Lucy with a light seda-
tive, Willow watched the dog slowly close her
eyes, and rubbed her head to make sure she
was falling asleep. 'There she goes.' Picking up the shaver, she removed the hair from
both hind paws.

Carter made an incision in the right one,
and another, to remove the dewclaw from the
uninjured foot.

Passing him the suture needle and thread,
Willow checked Lucy's breathing and heart.
'All good.' She knew it would be, but regular
checks saved being caught out by an unexpected problem.

'Bowl.'

She held it out for Carter to drop the needle into.

'Scalpel.'

She opened the pack and placed a new
blade in his outstretched hand.

His moves were precise, no extra cutting
where it wasn't needed. 'This is going to need
internal suturing where the tendon was torn
when the dewclaw was pulled.'

She liked that he explained what he was
doing. Not all vets did and, for her, knowing the details satisfied her thirst for more
knowledge. Sometimes she had wondered if
she should stop wandering and study to be-

come a vet. Having received a large payout after the accident, she had the funds to cover the years it would take to qualify so if it was what she truly wanted, she knew she'd do it. Just not yet.

Don't leave it too long, said her alter ego. Then she glanced at Carter, and the urge to stop moving around hit her hard. To stay and put down roots, to live in one place year in, year out. Get a pup. Have a man to go home to every day. What would that be like?

Carter looked up at her. 'You all right?'

Not at all. 'Couldn't be better,' she lied. More to herself than Carter, she admitted silently.

'For a moment there I thought you were going to say you couldn't watch while I do this op.' He looked baffled.

As well he should. 'I've never once felt unable to watch an operation, and this is a very minor one. For me, not Lucy.'

'That's what I thought.' He returned to tidying up Lucy's paw.

Willow continued monitoring their patient, and wishing she knew where all these thoughts about settling down, training as a vet and starting a new life were coming from. She couldn't blame Carter for it all.

'Want a coffee before our next case?'

Carter asked as she laid Lucy back in the cage a little while later.

'I'll give it a miss and take Axel for a quick walk.' She needed fresh air without Carter nearby. Working with him was proving harder than she'd experienced with other vets. She was constantly aware of him, kept watching his hands as he worked on an animal, and listened to his voice, and wondered what it might be like to make love with him.

Damn this, she was going to have to tell him she didn't need a partner for the wedding. She could not carry on pretending she didn't want more from him. Those kisses had sent her to the edge, waking her up in unexpected ways that had her wondering if she might struggle to pack her bags when it came time to go.

'Back here in ten minutes.'

'Sure.' She was very aware of his scrutiny as she walked out of the door. He wasn't happy she wasn't joining him in the tearoom. She wasn't either, but she had to get away, if only for a brief break. 'Come on, Axel. We haven't got long.' The pup seemed reluctant to leave his cosy bed, which was unlike him. She gave the lead a light tug. 'Move it, fella.'

He whined as he stepped closer to her.

'Axel? What's up?' As she ran her hand

over his hindquarter where Carter had re-located his displaced hip it felt wrong. As though he'd dislocated it again. How, when he was in a cage, unable to do anything very active? 'Carter,' she called, not wanting to leave the pup for a moment.

He loomed in the doorway. 'Problem?'

'I think Axel's hip's come out of the socket. But I can't see how that could happen. It was fine when I put him in here.'

Carter was at her side in an instant, running his hand over the spot where her hand lay. 'You're right. Did you take him for a walk this morning?'

She nodded. 'We went round the block for about twenty minutes. I keep the walks short at the moment. He's still tender.'

'Did he trip or fall?'

'Not that I— Hang on. A kid on a bike raced past us really close and Axel jerked sideways. He got a fright, I think, hadn't seen the kid coming. But he didn't seem bothered at the time.'

'Didn't limp? More than he has been?'

She swore. And met Carter's eye. 'Yes, he was limping more than usual. On and off. Sometimes he appeared fine, then it would be noticeable. I didn't think there was a problem.' What sort of nurse did that make her?

One distracted by too many thoughts about Carter, that was what.

Carter placed his hand on her shoulder, squeezed and let go. 'Stop it. You're being hard on yourself. It wouldn't be the first time someone's been caught out like that. Just the jerking away from the cycle would've hurt him, and made him limp on and off. To suspect he'd dislocated the joint you'd have needed more to go on.'

'You're being kind.'

'No one's perfect, Willow.' He stood up, lifting Axel with him. 'I'll give him something for the pain, and we'll get an image of the hip to see if there's more going on than I first thought. Anything else will have to wait until after the other animals have been dealt with.'

'He'll be fine in the cage with the pain under control,' she agreed, not wanting them to wait another minute. But it wasn't her place to prioritise patients. Nor could she find a valid reason to argue with Carter's decision other than she didn't want Axel waiting. There was no denying how much the pup had got to her. Just as well he'd be going home next week.

'I know you want me to put him first, but the owners of our other patients want the same for theirs, and some of them are more urgent.' There was nothing but understanding in Carter's face.

The warmth in his voice and eyes nearly undid her resolve to put some space between them. A solution to her mixed-up hormones and mind that she hadn't got around to admitting and putting into practice yet. He was almost too good to be true. Almost.

'I'll get the coffees while you give him something for the pain.' She'd drink hers in here where she could watch over Axel until it was time to prepare the next animal, Rusty, for a hernia op.

In about five minutes, she grimaced as she poured the coffees. At least time flew by in here. The morning would be over before she knew it and she could get that important space from Carter—that she'd no doubt spend thinking about him and his kisses. Or considering how to tell him she had changed her mind about him going to the wedding with her.

'I keep meaning to ask you about the wedding,' he said as she passed him a full mug. 'Is it smart or casual dress?'

Opportunity knocked, and she couldn't take it. He'd be hurt if she told him not to bother after they'd been getting on so well, to the point of sharing hot kisses. Besides, as much as she should probably go alone, she couldn't find it in her to do so. Not because Dave needed putting in his place any more, but because she enjoyed Carter's company far more than she'd have thought possible and very much wanted more of it.

'Smart casual,' she said, and found herself laughing despite her confusion. 'You don't have to wear a suit, but shorts and tee shirt isn't acceptable.'

His hand was up in a stop sign. His mouth was split into a friendly grin. 'I do understand smart casual. I have a wardrobe full of it. There're plenty of suits too.'

Her mouth watered at the thought of Carter all dressed up in a suit and tie, highly polished shoes adding the final touches. 'Feel free to wear one if you like. You obviously have a thing for good clothes.'

'One of my quirks.'

She couldn't wait to find out more. Heat filled her face. He did that to her without even trying. Or had he been teasing her? She didn't look, instead said, 'Time to get Rusty sorted.'

'I'll stick with Axel for a few more minutes.' There was laughter in his voice, making him sexier than ever.

So he had been stirring her. Waiting for a reaction? He wasn't getting one. 'Good for you.'

'What are you up to for the rest of the weekend?'

'I'm trying to arrange to see Mrs Burnside with Axel tomorrow morning. I'm also hitting the mall for a bit of shopping later today.' Did he have something in mind?

'I suggest you don't take Axel for walks until his hip's settled down again.'

No exciting invitation to join him. 'I don't intend to. What are you up to?' she couldn't resist asking.

'I'm heading to the farm tomorrow afternoon. I've got to do the annual clostridial dosage for the bulls.'

'Sounds like fun. Not.' They were such opposites. She didn't do settled down while he didn't do going off to any place that tickled his interest. She was a townie through and through. He was a country guy despite the fact he lived in town. So he was safe with her. This sense of wanting him was only physical and would pass.

'You can always come and help.' He grinned. 'It's not the most exciting way to spend an afternoon but we could have dinner after. Axel could lie on the deck with my two geriatrics.'

So he wanted to spend more time with her. Or was she reading too much into this? Probably. There weren't a lot of signs to go by. Could be she was putting too much of her own fears on Carter? Since the accident she had learned to see people more clearly, no longer take them at face value. 'It would be a way to get to know my wedding partner better.' So much for telling him he wasn't going with her. That problem had been taken out of her hands. A chill had lifted, leaving her warm and happy. 'Time to get our next patient on the table, and Axel under the scanner.'

'Willow, I'd like you to meet my mum and dad.' Aware of the tension ramping up in her stance, Carter placed his arm around her shoulders and drew her nearer to him and closer to his parents. It must be hard meeting people for the first time when often the first thing they'd notice would be her prosthesis, yet she didn't go out of her way to hide it. More points to Willow because obviously it was still confronting for her. 'Josie and Charlie.'

Mum stepped up, her usual friendly smile

in place. 'Hello, Willow. I'm glad to meet you. I hope Carter doesn't intend for you to dose the bulls.'

'Wouldn't put it past him.' Dad held his hand out to Willow. 'Hi, it's good to see you out here. You're a vet nurse, I hear.'

She shook his father's hand and nodded. 'That's right, but vaccinating bulls is not on my list of favourite things to do. It was definitely not my reason for coming today.'

Wonder what was, Carter thought. Not that he was asking. It was good enough she'd come with him. 'Let's get the dogs sorted and then deal with the bulls so I can take you for a meal afterwards.'

'You're not joining the family for dinner?' his mother asked, looking a bit miffed. 'We'd love for you to be there, Willow.'

He hadn't wanted to overwhelm Willow with everyone this early on. Who knew if they'd get to a point where his family was a part of their picture? And now he'd seen an interested glint in his mother's eyes as she looked at Willow he knew they had to leave as soon as possible. She'd be reading way too much into the fact he'd brought a woman out here for a few hours. If his mother was doing that, he'd hate to think what everyone else would come up with. 'I—'

'That'd be lovely, thank you, Josie.' Willow had beat him to it, surprising the hell out of him with her easy acceptance.

It wasn't how he'd intended the afternoon playing out. But it could be that it'd work out for the best. He was stepping outside his comfort zone so why not test the waters with his family? They understood him more than anybody. If Willow could say yes, then so could he. 'That's taken care of, then, thanks, Mum.'

Mum gave him a wink and headed inside.

'Where do we put the dogs?' Willow asked him.

'On the front deck. Mine won't need tying up but Axel should be. He'll probably try following you.' He opened the back of his ute. 'We've got an extra pup, Dad. Willow's dog-sitting for a few days.'

Once the dogs were sorted they headed across to the stock pens where his father and brothers had put the bulls earlier.

Willow was looking around as she walked beside him. 'Don't laugh but I've never been on a farm before. This looks beautiful with the paddocks stretching so far.'

'Are you serious? Where have you been?' Knock his socks off. If he'd been wearing any. 'You really are a city girl through and through.'

'Don't say I didn't warn you.'

'I didn't figure you meant you'd never been beyond the towns and cities you've been living in.'

'Of course I have, but seeing the countryside from a bus or car is quite different from standing on the land surrounded by grass and fences and cattle. It's awesome.' She hugged herself. 'An eye-opener. I like it.'

So did he. He was giving Willow a new experience and turned out she enjoyed it. 'Wait till we get to the pens and I start injecting the bulls. Then you'll hear roars like you've never heard.'

On his other side his father was chuckling softly. 'Interesting.'

Carter suspected his dad was referring to Willow and where she fitted into his life.

Wrong, Dad, wrong.

Or was he? Willow was the first woman he'd ever brought home to meet his family since Cassandra. Not that he'd brought Willow here with that in mind, but naturally coming to the farm meant meeting them. It hadn't occurred to him his parents would see anything in it. How blind could he be? Of course they would. His brothers and their wives weren't going to be any different.

'How many bulls are you vaccinating?' Willow asked.

'Six,' Dad answered. 'From both farms. I don't know what Carter's told you, but his brothers run the show. Cameron took over the family farm from me, and Calvin bought the one next door. It means everyone's on hand for the jobs that need more than one person to deal with.'

'A strong family unit,' she commented with a glance at him.

Carter felt his heart squeeze with affection. 'We get along most of the time.'

'Brothers being what they are, that's not every minute of every day,' Dad added. 'But nothing usually hinders them from getting things straightened out when need be.'

'Sounds like me and my brother. We're close, but don't always see eye to eye.' Her arm rubbed his and there was a soft smile on her face. She was happy.

Which made him more ecstatic. He wasn't quite sure why he'd invited her here when he'd be doing vet work. It was more like another day at the office than a date, which could explain it. He wanted to put the brakes on whatever it was growing between them, while at the same time the urge to leap in and take Willow with him wherever he went was growing every day. 'He's a city slicker too?'

'Absolutely. He hasn't travelled half as much as me though. He works for a mega company in central Sydney, lives in an apartment nearby, and socialises in the same area.'

Carter shook his head. He could not imagine being surrounded by multi-storeyed buildings twenty-four-seven. 'The few times I've been to Sydney I couldn't wait to get out again. All the people, traffic, ghastly air—it's unreal.'

'It's in my blood,' she said as she looked at him. This time there was no smile, more a warning in her voice.

He got it. They were poles apart when it came to lifestyles. Southport was a town, but nothing like the massive city Sydney was. He only had to drive a few kilometres and he was in the countryside. Or at the beach. It would take hours on the road to get to a paddock on the outskirts of Sydney. It wasn't for him.

Therein lay their differences. The big ones anyway. He'd better remember that whenever he thought they were getting close. Typical. When he finally became interested in a woman, she was all wrong for him.

It doesn't feel wrong.
Shut up.

'She's got your number, hasn't she?' Mum said to him three hours later as he stacked the dishwasher after dinner.

'That's how she stays in touch, Mum.' Damn it. He shouldn't have brought Willow out here. If only he'd thought it through. Of course he'd get digs from his mother, who wanted so much for him to settle down and have a family. The only surprise had been no one else had had a crack at him.

'Relax, Carter. I like her. There are no pretences about her. She calls a spade a spade.'

'She's had a hard time. But she doesn't rush to tell me all her woes.'

'Another point in her favour. You haven't asked?'

'You raised us to be respectful, remember?' He had been nosy enough to look online though. It did make him feel a little guilty, although it was a fact of the modern world that if you wanted to know something you typed it in.

'That we did. Glad it stuck.' His mother smiled softly. 'Bring her out here again.'

'We'll see.'

'You're cautious?'

'Why wouldn't I be?'

Laughter came through the doors opening onto the deck, Willow's the loudest of them all. Warmth wound through him, touched him in places he hadn't felt anything for a long time.

'That's why,' Mum said, watching him closely. 'She's got to you.'

'I'm not rushing this,' he said, harsher than intended. 'It's early days.'

'Enjoy them.'

He watched his mother walk outside. 'I am, Mum. So much I'm worried I mightn't know how to stop,' he said under his breath.

'Feel like a stroll on the beach?' Willow asked Carter as they got closer to her street. She wasn't ready to head inside and listen to her flatmates talking non-stop about anything and everything. Or asking about her afternoon. Let's face it, she wasn't ready to say goodnight to Carter.

'Sure. Why not? I think Axel should stay in the ute. He's not entirely comfortable with that hip.'

They'd left his dogs at the farm. 'I agree.' She'd agree to anything. Carter hadn't hesitated in going along with her suggestion. It had been an interesting afternoon and eve-

ning with his family. They were lovely people. So easy to get along with, and none of
them had made her feel awkward. Could it
be she was moving past her hang-ups about
her leg? If so, she owed Carter a big thank
you because this had all started when she'd
met him.

They held hands as they wandered along
on the edge of the sea where the sand was
damp and solid. The sun had dropped below
the horizon and the temperature had fallen
with it but the salty air was still warm. A
little zing was going on where their palms
and fingers connected, sending vibes streaming throughout her. Breathing deep, Willow
absorbed the happiness radiating out of her.
What a day. Could they have more? A fling
with Carter was so, so tempting. 'I like your
family.' Nothing to do with a fling.

'They like you too.'

They'd welcomed her with open arms, and
even given her the same cheeky comments
they handed out to Carter from time to time.
When one of the children had asked her what
happened to her leg, she'd been so relaxed it
hadn't been awkward to tell the lad, 'I was
in an accident and it had to be cut off.' When
Mickey had then asked if it hurt, he'd been
told by his father that was enough and to go

get another bag of crisps. It had been so normal that she hadn't wanted to run and hide. Much like spending time with her own family.

A longing for her parents filled her. They were there at the end of the phone any time she wanted to talk. If she dropped in at the house in Sydney they'd all pick up where they'd left off last time she'd visited. But it was the everyday stuff, being a short drive away from them, sharing a meal and laughs, looking out for each other, that she hadn't had in a long time.

Carter nudged her. 'Where have you gone?'

'Home,' she replied instantly. That was how relaxed she was around this man. Her guard dropped whenever they were alone.

'You miss your family?'

'I'm only just realising how much. Seeing your parents and brothers, and how close you all are.' She shrugged. 'It brought back memories of good times.'

He wrapped an arm around her waist and drew her nearer as they kept strolling along the water's edge. 'What's changed?'

'Me.'

Carter didn't push her for more. Nor did he let her go.

She snuggled closer. If she explained he'd

understand why she wasn't staying on after her contract ran out even though he'd made her start wishing for more.

'The accident that took my leg happened when I was out training with a group of professional cyclists. A truck jackknifed into us, causing mayhem. My two best friends were killed instantly. I can't forget the screams and shouts and the smell. It's something I haven't been able to put behind me. Sometimes I see Dee and Jess in the dark of night and I think of everything they've missed out on because of one man's mistake.'

The words poured over her lips. She hadn't said as much to anyone for years. 'I don't want that to happen to me. I also think if I have all these amazing experiences then somehow they'll know and get something from them too.' Now he'd think she was nuts. She shrugged again. 'It's how it is. I can't help it.'

Carter stopped and turned to her, his hands taking her face ever so gently and tipping her head back enough to meet her gaze. 'You are amazing. No one would come through what you've just told me and not have fears and pain from losing your friends. Yet you still manage to smile and laugh, and help others, including people's pets. Don't ever underestimate your strength and courage.' His eyes were moist as he spoke softly. 'Trust me on this.'

A solitary tear escaped to roll down her cheek. No one had ever said something so beautiful to her. Not even her family when they were trying to help her put the pieces of her life back together. 'Carter—'

'Shh…' He leaned in and pressed a light kiss on her lips. 'Keep taking care of yourself, Willow. You're doing a great job.' Then his kiss deepened, filling her with hope and longing and wonder.

She clung to him and kissed him in return. A thank-you kiss, then an I'm-lost-in-you kiss. She pulled back and gazed up into those intense eyes. 'Take me to bed, Carter.'

This time he didn't tell her to 'shh'. Instead he took her hand and walked them quickly back to his vehicle and drove to his house.

Braking outside his house, Carter shoved open his door and dashed around to open Willow's. He scooped her into his arms, kicked the door shut, and raced inside. His mind was a blur of need and caring and relief at hearing her story from her and pride in this amazing woman. He wanted to wipe

away for ever the pain he'd heard in her voice
and seen in her face.

Lying her on his bed, he lowered down
beside her and took her in his arms, wound
his legs around hers. Felt the solid prosthesis against his shin and smiled. 'This is you.
Willow.' The woman turning his world upside down, causing him to rethink so much.

Her hands skimmed his butt. Her mouth
caressed his chin. Her eyes didn't leave his.
'Thank you.'

Two little words that he knew meant so
much coming from Willow. He accepted her
as she was. No ifs or buts. Why wouldn't
he? She was gorgeous in so many ways. 'No
more talking.' He followed through by putting his mouth to good use, kissing first those
delightful lips, then trailing his mouth down
her neck to the vee of her shirt that led to her
breasts and beyond. He took his time, undoing clothes, tasting, licking that sensual body,
enjoying her soft skin, arousing them both
as he went. He unstrapped her prosthesis as
though he'd been doing it for years, making
it a sexy act as his hands and lips touched her
skin, heated her some more. Then he reached
into the bedside drawer for a condom.

Willow's hands were finding parts of him
that hadn't been touched in a long time,

winding him tighter by the minute until he thought he'd explode with need. 'Stop,' he growled against her stomach.

She increased the pace.

Taking her hands, he held them above her head and continued lighting her fire.

'Carter, slow down. I want to take in every moment, every sensation, everything.'

With his free hand, he undid the zip on her pants and tugged them down enough to give him access to her sex. His fingers touched, seeking her heat, her moistness.

'Fine.' She writhed up against him, pulled her hands free and reached for him, sliding those hot palms up and down his length. Her breaths were short and sharp. Her hips pushed up against him, inviting him to join her.

How could he not? He was tight, hot and fizzing. He had to have her, to share this with her, to know her completely. Lifting himself over her, he slid inside the heat, and gasped. Pulling back, he pressed deeper, again and again, until Willow was crying out her release and shuddering all around him.

Carter fell into the wonder of Willow and knew no more.

When he next opened his eyes, she was lying on her side next to him, her head in her hand as she watched over him. A large smile split her face, and there was a sparkle in her eyes he'd never seen before.

'Hi,' she whispered.

'That was something else.'

'It sure was.'

'I think we've been heading towards this since the moment I opened the clinic door to you holding the pup in your arms.'

Her smile got even wider. 'I can't argue with that.'

So they were on the same page. That made it all so much easier. 'Come here.' He reached for her, wound his body around hers, and held tight. Willow was coming to mean so much and he couldn't imagine letting go of her. But that day would come. She'd been up front about not staying for ever. In the meantime he'd make the most of whatever they had together. 'Want to stay the rest of the night?'

'Can't think of anywhere I'd rather be.' Then she shot upright. 'Axel's still in the ute.' She hadn't thought about him once.

'Relax. He'll be fine. I'll go and bring him inside. There's a spare bed he can use.'

Lying back on the pillows, she laughed. Wow. Making love had flipped her world upside down and all around. It was the best thing to happen in a long time.

CHAPTER FIVE

WILLOW PUT THE phone in her pocket and returned to the staff room where everyone was gearing up for the day by downing coffee. 'That was Miriam Burnside. Her daughter arrived from London yesterday to spend a month with her and will be in to collect Axel later today.' She was going to miss the little guy. He'd snuck in under her radar when she wasn't looking. Much like another male she was getting to know too well.

Carter was watching her as she sat down across the table from him, sympathy in his gaze. She didn't like how well he read her sometimes. Then again, it was a novelty and there was a lot of positive good about it. He understood her. He said, 'I suppose that's best.' His gaze was telling her he knew she wasn't going to like handing Axel over.

'We'll have to find another pup for Willow to mother,' Joe said. 'You're good at it,' he told her.

'It would only be upset when the time came for me to leave.' Something that was looking harder by the day. Getting intimate with Carter had brought down more barriers around her heart. But not so many that she could risk staying put. That need to remain footloose and fancy free was non-negotiable. It kept her sane.

No one was talking.

Willow looked around and found everyone watching her. 'What?'

Kathy broke the silence. 'There's a possibility that Abbie won't be returning at the end of her leave. You'd be the first person we'd offer a permanent position to.'

A chill settled over her. Crunch time. When she and Carter were having a great time she had to make a decision about them and their future. *It's a wake-up call.* A reminder that whatever was going on with them, she still wouldn't be here for ever. Not that she'd forgotten, but over the days since the weekend it had been too easy to pretend she was in a different world. 'I'd have to say no.'

Carter flinched.

Sorry, but you knew that.

Hopefully he hadn't decided she'd change

her mind if they got seriously involved. The point was, that wasn't going to happen no matter how close they became.

'Let's wait until nearer the time when we do know what Abbie's decided,' Seamus said quietly. 'It's still a while away.'

'Good idea,' Joe added.

No, it wasn't. She wouldn't change her mind. Even if she wanted to. Her fingers clenched, unclenched. She did not want to stop moving. Life would catch up. It might have already. In the shape of one tall, hunky male sitting opposite her, watching her. Did he honestly expect her to change her way of life so soon? It wasn't possible. She might have the hots for him, but she was not falling in love.

Carter remained quiet. Was he regretting everything?

Under the table Willow crossed her fingers in the hope that over the coming weeks he'd still want to spend time with her outside here. It was unfair, but they were having fun. By being himself and accepting her for herself, he was showing she could have a life similar to what had once been her norm. But, and here was the big problem, she still didn't believe she was ready to hand over her heart completely. Because it would have to be all or nothing, and she was opting for nothing. To be able to never worry about losing him if she loved him would be impossible. She was no longer blind to reality. *Her* reality, probably, but it was still very true and unnerving.

Carter stood up. 'Right, let's get the show on the road.'

'Before we do, I was going to ask if you could swap weekends with me, Carter,' Seamus asked. 'I've got a family shindig happening and it works out to be the same weekend I'm on call.'

Here we go. Seamus was talking about the weekend of the wedding. Willow's lungs were on hold as everyone waited for Carter's answer. *Will he? Won't he?*

He glanced at her, a bemused look on his handsome face.

'It's okay, I can change with you if Carter isn't available,' Joe said.

Will he? Won't he?

Finally he smiled at her, and turned to Seamus. 'Sorry, mate, but I'm going to a wedding.'

Willow sank back into her chair. They were still on. Not that she'd really thought he'd change his mind once he'd committed to going. Still her day had just got brighter, and it had already been beaming until a few minutes ago. She flicked Carter a lopsided smile.

Got one in return.

The doorbell buzzed.

'There goes the peace and quiet.' Joe stood.

'What's first up for us?' Willow asked Carter when they were in the operating room. Despite that blip in the tearoom, looking at him sent spears of lust throughout her body, reminding her of their lovemaking on Sunday night. There hadn't been a chance for a repeat performance since then as Carter had various things on and she'd spent an evening with Pip and her friends again celebrating the upcoming nuptials.

The door closed with a small click. 'This.' He took her in his arms and lowered his mouth to cover hers. 'You talk too much.' Then he proceeded to kiss her senseless.

When they finally came up for air, she started to laugh. This was so freeing. Carter literally took the air out of her lungs. 'I need a cold shower before we begin operating.'

'You think?' He laughed, and moved away to bring up the computer screen with the notes about the Labrador with a cancerous growth on its lung.

Another morning, another line up of animals needing their help. More hours working with Carter. She'd be in here with Seamus in the afternoon, but right now this was perfect.

You're already ignoring the warnings that lit up when it was suggested you might like to sign up permanently.

The steel bowl slipped from her fingers, clattered onto the floor. It was too easy to forget her own rules while in Carter's company. Her smile faltered.

'Willow? You all right?' He was at her side, reaching down for the bowl.

Was she? When her stomach was melting and her head spinning just from looking at him? 'I think so.'

'I think so, too,' he said softly. 'Now let's get on with why we're here.'

Would that help solve her dilemma? They were having a fling. Nothing more. Unless she called a halt now, she might as well make the most of it and enjoy every moment she got to spend with Carter. He was sublime in bed—and out of it. She lov... Liked him very, very much.

'Willow, Mrs Burnside's daughter, Avril, is here.' Kathy appeared in the doorway. 'Do you want to take Axel out to her?'

Not really. She'd rather hide and pretend she never knew a loving pup named Axel.

But she wasn't a coward. 'Be there in a minute.' She couldn't leave the operating room until Carter had finished suturing the incision he'd made to remove a bone fragment on the Alsatian's hip.

Carter paused with one suture to go. 'Want me to do it?'

Yes. 'No, thanks. It wouldn't be fair on Axel not to give him a goodbye hug, would it?'

'You're going to miss him.'

'Unfortunately, yes.' More than she'd have believed. The young fella had sneaked in under her radar and most mornings when she'd got up to take him for a walk before they came into the clinic she'd had a sense of fulfilling one of her dreams. The time looking after him had turned her soft about having a pet. Time to be strong.

Carter made another neat suture, cut the thread. 'But you can't say you're sorry you took him in.'

'True.' She stared at the dog he was finishing up on. 'I've really enjoyed taking him out and about, having him sit on the deck nearby when I'm relaxing at the end of the day.'

'One of the things you'll do when you settle in one place, then, is get a dog.'

'Possibly.' Unlikely if the ache already

starting in her heart was anything to go by. She put the bowl in the sink to wash and drew a breath. She'd better go and hand Axel over.

Carter carefully lifted his patient and took him through to place in a cage Willow had prepared earlier.

She followed and picked up a lead before heading over to Axel, who immediately stood up, his tail wagging furiously. 'Sorry, fella. We're not going for a walk. But better news. You're going home and your mum will join you in a couple of days. How's that?'

She rubbed his familiar head and swallowed hard. Damn it but she'd gone soft over this pup in such a short time. She turned her head away and sniffed as quietly as possible. It wasn't a good look if anyone else noticed, especially Carter. He'd think she was softening. She wasn't. She couldn't afford to. It was too risky.

First a dog, then what? A man? Carter? Because he was slipping in under her defences. Not even slowly. He'd caught her attention from the moment he opened the clinic's door the night she brought Axel here. Carter and Axel kind of went hand in paw when it came to her and her feelings. She was pretending

Carter meant nothing more than amazing kisses and crazy hot sex, when really it was his kindness, understanding and a whole heap of more good things that were dragging her out of her deep place and waking her up. Which meant it was time to stand tall, strong, and alone.

Carter walked out to the waiting room behind Willow and Axel. She was hurting. Denying it with every determined step and in the way her chin was high, but there was no doubt she was not enjoying this moment.

'Avril?' She approached the only woman in the room.

'Hi. Are you Willow? Mum said you found her pup and had been taking care of him ever since. She's so grateful, believe me. It was really kind of you. Thank you so much.'

When Willow didn't reply immediately, Carter stepped up. 'Yes, this is Willow, and she has been looking after Axel. He's doing very well. I'm Carter, the vet who treated him. I need to fill you in on the details if you've got a moment.'

'Of course.'

While he filled the woman in, he kept an eye on Willow, who kept touching the pup,

her face determinedly emotionless. Not so
her eyes. They were filled with longing. 'Ba-
sically Axel's good for anything in modera-
tion.'

'I'll fix up any expenses incurred now.'
Avril bent down to pat Axel and got a wary
stare for her trouble. 'Hey, Axel, it's all right.
I'm taking you home. No more sitting in a
cage at the vet's.'

Axel pressed into Willow's knee. The pup
had long ago worked out to sit or stand on her
left side, away from the prosthesis.

Willow's hand found his head and rubbed
softly. 'There you go. Avril's going to look
after you, fella. You'll be fine.' Her voice
wobbled.

Carter held back from reaching to hug her.
Wrong place, wrong time.

When Avril crossed to the desk and handed
Kathy her credit card, Willow reached lower
and patted the pup along his back. 'You're
a great pup. You be good for Avril, okay?'
Then she stood up, handed Carter the lead
and headed out to the back of the building.

He ached to follow but he was stuck until
Avril took Axel, and she was talking to
Kathy, seeming as if she had all day. Time
to step up and get things rolling. Apart from
wanting to be with Willow, he knew there

more animals awaiting his attention out the back. Might be the way to go, keep on operating and letting Willow settle into the routine. Helping other animals would relax her some.

She was well ahead of him with that idea, having got the table cleaned and ready for Moxy, a Persian cat needing to be spayed as she was in early pregnancy and the owner didn't want more kittens. She hadn't even wanted the cat to ever fall pregnant but had been putting off this operation until it was too late.

Willow had the cage open and was lifting the cat out. 'Here we go.'

The cat had been given a drug to quieten her. Now he had to administer something stronger to be able to intubate her and keep her asleep throughout the operation. Carter scrubbed his hands, pulled on gloves, and joined Willow, who was *too* busy monitoring the cat. She hadn't stopped feeling sad.

That urge to hug her returned. He pushed it away. 'Ready.'

She handed him the anaesthetic drug. 'This is one cute cat.'

'Apparently some male cat thought so too,' he replied, trying for light and cheery, and was rewarded with a light chuckle and a small smile.

'Most likely a stray. Though there might be a frustrated pedigree living in the neighbourhood that thought Moxy was the best thing out.'

'The fun of romance, eh?' he quipped, then held his breath. Hopefully Willow didn't read anything about their relationship into that.

'Can't say I've thought about cats having romantic liaisons,' she murmured as she handed him the tube to slide down the cat's throat.

With the tube in place, Carter watched Willow shave the cat's abdominal area. As always, she was confident and fast. As her hand slid the razor over the skin the slump in her shoulders disappeared and the tension in her face relaxed. She was moving past watching Axel walk out of her life. For now at least.

What would it take for her to settle down? Maybe have a pet or two? Start a long-term relationship? Have a home that she could call hers? His heart felt heavy for what she was missing out on because of that accident. Surely she wouldn't keep moving on every time she started to feel comfortable for the rest of her life? That would be a waste of opportunities for love and a family. Wasn't he doing much the same? He might be settled here but he wasn't exactly opening up to love and a family.

His gaze followed those hands now wiping an antiseptic cloth over the cat's skin. Hands he could all too easily recall on his skin, making him hot with anticipation. Opening him up to a longing for so much more. With Willow? Or because of Willow? Either, or.

Didn't matter. He was not getting serious about her. It might be too late. Then he'd have to back away, take a few breaths, and get back on track. Falling in love again was not an option if he wanted to feel safe. Falling in love with Willow was definitely off the menu because there was only one way she was going and that was out of town come the end of March. There'd be no stopping her. She'd never said otherwise.

His incision into the cat's abdomen was quick and precise, exposing only what he required for the procedure. Fixing animals physically was what he was good at. Giving them back to their owners in better condition than they'd arrived. Making them well again. Or euthanising them when nothing else could save them. That was the downside to the job, even when justified. The heartbreak in owners' faces always tightened his chest. But he loved vet work because he loved animals.

They were strong and adoring, just as he tried to be with the humans in his life. He glanced over at Willow. He could be strong for her, share the load she carried on those slight shoulders. Make her happier, love her.

No, not love. He might feel he was getting closer to being ready for that, but close wasn't enough. He had to be all in or not within sight. So he'd stick with their fling and hope that he'd get over these new—*admit it*—exhilarating emotions filling him with wonder every day since he'd met Willow.

Concentrating on the operation, Carter soon forgot what he'd been thinking about, and removed the uterus and its unwanted litter. He had tried to persuade the owner to let Moxy have the kittens before he did this, but the woman wasn't having a bar of that. Nothing he could but go ahead with the op. Did Moxy understand she was pregnant? Would she feel any sense of loss when she came to? Questions he often asked himself as he did the job and had yet to find answers to. No harder than some of the questions about himself.

'Feel like going to the pub after work tonight?' That was not a question he'd known was coming. Now he held his breath, waiting for Willow's answer.

A tray with threaded needles appeared beside his patient. The steel bowl containing the scalpel and body part was removed.

His chest began aching as he tried, and failed, to exhale.

Answer me, will you? Say, yes, that'd be great. Say anything so I can start breathing again.

Picking up a needle, he looked at Willow.

A frown marred her forehead. Her mouth was tight.

Okay, so she didn't want to join him for a beer. Fair enough. Why not say so?

Then she shook her head and looked directly at him. 'Thanks, but I've got a few chores to do.' Unfortunately for Willow, a red hue rose up her neck to her cheeks. She didn't tell fibs very well.

He'd be generous, let her off. That was her way of trying to let him down gently, he supposed. 'That's fine. Another time.' Fingers crossed. He wasn't ready to finish their fling. Might never be. No, he'd already accepted they weren't in it for the long haul. Willow's move might be for the best. Done and dusted. No more of those earth-shattering kisses. No more making love with her. He should be grateful she'd had the guts to turn his invitation down. But he wasn't. He was gutted. Spending time with Willow was the best thing to happen in a very long time.

'Sure.' She went back to handing him needles and watching the cat's monitor.

He got on with suturing the incision and trying to swallow his disappointment.

Carter wasn't happy with her for saying no to going to the pub. She was sorry, but she wasn't changing her mind. She needed space, needed to get back to normal, which meant running solo with only a few times out. They'd had a fling, short and amazing, but now she had to call it quits before she found she couldn't move on from Carter.

If she felt disconsolate about handing Axel over after little more than a week, then how would she feel when it came time to leave Southport and Carter? Axel was adorable. Carter was... Well, he was everything she'd dared to dream a man might be and some. He listened to her without interruption or adding his own take on her opinions. He made her weak at the knees with his kisses. He seemed to understand why she lived the way she did.

Placing Moxy in her cage, she straightened up and rubbed her lower back where it ached from too much standing at the operating table. She could go on and on about

Carter and all the reasons why she was a little bit in love with him. A love that needed knocking into place before it became any stronger and had her making decisions she might later come to regret. Ten days was not long enough to know if he was as wonderful as she believed. Certainly not long enough to make life-changing choices about where she lived and with who.

Closing the cage, she crossed to the next one where a dog lay sleeping due to a light tranquilliser in readiness for an op on his ear to make drainage easier. Spaniels' long hairy ears made it difficult to easily clear infections of the ear, and as they often got grass seeds caught in there, it was a common occurrence. A delicate procedure lay ahead and then he'd have to wear a plastic collar for a while to prevent him scratching at the surgical site.

More time for her spent working alongside the man turning her common sense to mush and having her wonder if it was possible to change her way of life and risk getting closer to him. Had she done the right thing by turning him down? Hell, yes. It was all about protecting herself. Absolutely essential.

'Come on, Perky, your turn.' Of course the spaniel couldn't hear her, but she always wondered if talking to the animals at this stage might somehow reach them and help with their mindset during the op. She was probably delusional, but she loved dogs and if she could reach them in any way then she would.

Carefully lifting the surprisingly heavy dog, she limped out of the room and into the operating room. Dang, but her knee hurt today. She hadn't done anything overly strenuous before coming to work, but some days were like that for no apparent reason. The joys of having a prosthesis.

'I'm operating on both ears,' Carter informed her as she placed Perky on the table before him. 'The owner agreed it's best because, while he's only had the left ear infected more than once, he's likely as not to have more in the right one at any stage.'

'Makes sense, and saves the little guy from coming back again.' His fur was soft under her hand. Quite a cutie, but then in her book all the dogs they saw were. 'You want me to hold the ear back while you operate?'

'I prefer that to pegging it. Less aching afterwards for him.'

'No problem.' Handing Carter the syringe of anaesthesia, she reached for the tube, ready for him to intubate Perky. She liked working with him. He didn't muck about getting ready or making incisions, just got on with the job so the animal wasn't kept unconscious any longer than absolutely necessary. Face it, she liked working, sharing a meal or sex, talking, laughing, with Carter. She'd said no to going to the pub tonight. Wise girl. Or not?

She was already missing spending that time with him when it would just be the two of them sitting on stools at a table, talking about anything that came to mind, unaware of the other patrons. It wasn't the same as being here where they had to concentrate on the operation and patient. Their breaks were with other staff as everyone came and went between jobs. She should've said yes. But then she did need to step back and think about her feelings for Carter and how far she intended to take them. It was only fair on Carter, and protection for herself.

'Are you on the rural roster tomorrow?'

'I am.' He didn't look her way. 'And Friday, since Seamus has an appointment in town in his lunch break and wouldn't be able to get back in time otherwise.'

Two days without Carter around the clinic. That should feel good, except it didn't. She knew she'd miss him. Which went to show she was doing the right thing staying away tonight. They'd only end up in bed and hyping up her feelings even more. 'Will you stay overnight at the farm?' She held Perky's left ear back as far as possible to expose the site Carter needed to work on.

'Probably. I always have an overnight pack in the ute in case I decide not to come back to town until the morning. It's no big deal if I manage to con dinner out of Mum.' He was shaving the small area he was going to cut, deft short strokes with the razor.

'I doubt it takes much conning.' His family were close and seemed to enjoy each other's company. Much like hers. Come to think of it, she owed her parents a call. It had been a couple of weeks since she'd last talked to them and they liked to know how she was getting on. She suspected they really wanted to find out if she'd met anyone exciting and was possibly considering staying put. Knowing she had no intentions of that didn't stop them hoping one day she would. They missed her and would love for her to return to Sydney, but if not there, then at least somewhere accessible by plane.

No fear of her going to the outback. Living in wide open spaces with few people about was not her style. She'd loved growing up in Sydney and cities were in her blood. Southport was very small in comparison but at least she had neighbours within a few metres of the house she shared, and there was a large mall up the road at Gold Coast, bars and takeaway food outlets everywhere.

'You're right, but it makes me feel better if I show I really want to be with them.' Finally he smiled. 'Families, eh? They keep us on our toes, and I like that. It makes me feel good.'

'Know what you mean. We're like that too. My brother did get a bit overprotective of me after the accident, but he learned to back off since it only made me tetchy. I think Mum and Dad wanted to wrap me up in cotton wool but somehow they refrained.'

'That must've been hard for them.'

'I reckon. It's why I call them regularly.' Though she had been remiss since meeting Carter. He distracted her so much. Not because she wasn't going to talk about him to her parents. She wasn't, but she could manage to avoid that while still keeping in touch. 'I'll phone them tonight, keep them up to date with what I've been doing.'

Carter seemed too focused on his work as he asked, 'Do they know you've been dog-sitting?'

'I haven't spoken to them since I started working here, but I'll fill them in tonight.'

It was easier now that Axel had gone home. They mightn't pick up on how she felt about the pup if he wasn't there staring at her with those big brown eyes.

'When did you last go home to see your folks?'

'I shot down to Sydney for a couple of nights after I finished at the Brisbane Clinic. It was great catching up with everyone. My brother has a new girlfriend, and, while that's nothing unusual, this time apparently he's completely smitten. Who knows what might come of it?'

It would be awesome if he fell in love and stopped being the playboy he'd earned a rep for. Sometimes she wondered if that had been his reaction to the crash that took the lives of her friends. He'd known them both a little, though hadn't been close. That day had affected so many people in lots of different ways, not only the ones directly involved or their family and friends.

'Sounds like you're hoping something will come of the relationship.' Was that a wistful question?

'I am.' Did Carter want a permanent relationship, despite what he'd told her about his fiancée leaving him and how he didn't think he could ever trust another woman? He probably did. She did. But she wasn't ready, and he'd said he wasn't either. Wasn't that true?

'Then here's hoping it comes to something.'

Willow smiled. Finally the sadness of saying goodbye to Axel had gone. That was what talking with Carter did, made her happy and relaxed. He had her number, for sure. Did she do the same to him? That was something she was not about to ask. If he said yes, she'd be confused about what to do going forward. Going forward when she'd said no to a drink? Okay, how about taking a break from him and seeing how she felt? But she already knew she was going to miss time with Carter outside the clinic. How could she not when she woke up every morning thinking about him? Excited to be seeing him at work?

'Thread more needles, will you? I'm getting through them.'

'Sorry, I didn't realise.' Earth to Willow. She should concentrate on what was important. Although wasn't thinking about Carter important?

The week dragged. Not so much at work but after hours. It was so unusual for Willow to feel time dragging by she wondered if she was coming down with something. It was more like an unrequited love bug, she thought with a sigh as she wandered around the mall with her flatmate on Sunday morning. There was nothing wrong with her health other than a heavy heart. Was she doing the right thing, keeping Carter out of her life other than as one of her bosses? It had to be, or why put up with feeling so down?

'Would a coffee put a smile on your face?' asked Lena, her flatmate.

'Sorry. I am being gloomy. My shout.' She had a couple of bags hanging from her hand after splashing out on a new swimsuit and some shoes.

'You're on. Why the mood when you've just bought the most amazing pair of shoes to wear to the wedding next week?'

Good point. 'They're cool, aren't they?' Red heels to match her dress. Not too high so she didn't make an ass of herself trying to keep her balance.

'You amaze me how you manage to walk on them.'

'I get wobbly at times. But hey, I like dressing up, and I'm not going to stop because I'm missing a foot.'

Lena laughed. 'Good excuse to cling to your partner when you're dancing. If he's hot and you want to get close, that is.'

'Oh, yeah.' Damn but she wished Carter were here and she could wrap her arms around him, hold him close and breathe him in. 'He is.'

'When do we get to meet this amazing man who's put sparks in your eyes?'

'Yes, well, I'm not seeing him other than at work at the moment.'

'Really? When you're going to the wedding with him? Doesn't make sense.'

Lena was right. It didn't. 'I don't want to get too involved. I'm heading away once this contract's up, remember?' Talk about a broken record. The same excuses every time she justified what she was doing. How about tossing caution to the wind and leaping in? She shivered. Scary. Too dangerous.

'You sure you want to do that?'

'What? Go someplace else and get to experience another country? Absolutely.' Did she though?

Of course she did. It was who she'd become.

Back at home Willow was restless. The shopping trip hadn't lifted her spirits as much as she'd hoped. Her head was still full of questions there were no answers for. None she'd consider likely anyway. 'I'm going for a swim,' she announced to anyone listening and changed into her swimsuit. The water would cool her skin if nothing else.

With the temperature in the high twenties, it was no surprise the beach was busy. Locals and tourists making the most of the perfect weather. Willow made her way down to the waterline, stripped off her shorts and tee shirt and hopped into the sea, leaving her crutch, towel and clothes on the sand. Getting in deep enough to float without stranding on the bottom, she lay on her back and stared up at the endless blue above while paddling slowly further out. This was magic. A great go-to place to be at. Even with kids yelling all around her and parents calling them back she could finally relax and breathe in fresh air. Salty and damp but free of problems.

What was Carter doing? Naturally he popped into her head the moment she relaxed. Was he at home or out at the farm with his family?

Don't go there, Willow. You'll only wind yourself up again.

Rolling over, she began to swim overarm, heading out to sea, leaving the crowd behind her. Left, right, her arms ploughed through the water. Left, right, again and again. Thinking of nothing, letting the water work its magic and the rhythm of her strokes take over. Finally she paused, treading water, and looked around. Being in the sea was one time when her body was free of difficulties. There was no need to fight to keep her balance. She felt whole.

Off she went again. Faster now, digging deeper with her hands on each stroke, churning through the sea, out to where kayakers and surfboard riders bobbed in the light waves waiting for a bigger one. It mightn't be great conditions for surfing but that didn't stop people coming out with their boards just in case. A couple of guys called hello when she stopped and dog-paddled while getting her breath back.

'Great day for it,' she answered. Whatever *it* was. At last she was happy. For the first time in days, since she'd turned down Carter's invitation, the tension that had gripped her was gone, worked out of her system with those precise, determined strokes through the water.

She turned for the beach and slowly swam back to shore where she stopped in deep enough water to stand on her foot and hop out onto the sand.

'You weren't a competitive swimmer in your past, by any chance?' Carter stood in front of her, two dogs sniffing around behind him and her crutch in his hand. 'You ate up the metres like you were on a stroll.'

'I took up swimming when I gave up cycling.' Sort of. She took her crutch and tucked it under her arm. How long had he been watching her? 'What brought you here?'

'I went by your place to see if you'd join me for a beer and Lena told me where to find you.'

He wanted to spend time with her. Yes. She'd have punched the air but it might make her look overly keen. The caution that had kept her from going out with him last week was still there, only quieter. 'I'd love a beer.' Reaching up, she brushed his mouth with hers. 'After I go home and change.'

His eyes cruised down her body, making her hot enough to want to dive back into the water. 'Do you have to?'

CHAPTER SIX

NO WONDER WILLOW was so lithe, Carter thought. He got tired just watching her swim. She'd headed straight out, away from the beach, going like a bat out of hell. Definitely one super-fit woman. 'I'm impressed,' he said as he drove towards the house she was living in.

'What with?' She sounded perplexed. But then she wasn't a mind-reader.

'Your level of fitness.'

'I always did a lot of training when I was into competitive cycling, and afterwards I kept going by swimming as much as possible to keep my damaged leg strong. Anyway, I can't imagine not exercising one way or another. It's what I've always done.'

'Makes sense. I can't see you ever slacking off.' He was not going swimming with her any time soon. Probably better not try hiking or tennis or any other sport either. She'd leave him for dead. So much for a prosthetic leg slowing her down. But then he'd known that from the get-go.

'Staying busy keeps me sane.' She laughed tightly, suggesting there was a hint of truth in those words. She really had had a hard time, but, hell, she was doing well.

'Describe sane,' he joked. Enough of being serious.

'Can't,' she retorted.

'Damn but I missed this.'

Her head spun around so she was staring at him. 'What?'

'The way we talk and tease each other and laugh. I'm always relaxed around you. It's like we clicked when I opened the door and there you were with Axel.'

Where did all that come from? It was like a torrent spilling out of him. It had to be said, no matter the risk. He had missed Willow so much over the past nights it was unbelievable. He had not believed he could ever feel this way again. To want to be with Willow all the time, not only at work. To share his thoughts on the day. To sit and enjoy a meal together. Just to be with her. That was why he'd gone to find her earlier. It underlined how much he missed her if he could toss caution to the wind.

She was still staring at him, but her face had softened and there was a hint of a smile at the corners of that beautiful mouth. 'Wow.'

He pulled to the side of the road. 'Yes, wow. Sorry if that's putting pressure on you, but it's the truth.' He hadn't been this open about his feelings since Cassandra. Another thing to credit Willow for. He was starting to feel again, and liking it—a lot.

She turned to look out of the window, her hands small fists against her thighs.

Placing one hand over them, Carter squeezed softly. 'It's okay. I'm not asking you to say anything you might later regret.'

Her hands straightened and turned over to hold his. 'I know what you mean by how well we get on. These last few nights have been kind of—empty.' That last word burst across her lips.

Warmth pushed throughout him. They were on the same page. Awesome. 'I get that it's quite frightening. For both of us. We've been protecting ourselves and don't know how to let go. Let's just go with the flow, enjoy our time together without putting too much pressure on ourselves.'

He hadn't realised how much he wanted that until he said those words. But it was true. It had been growing over the past days, this

longing to find a woman to be close to, and
that woman was Willow. If she'd have him.
It was early days, but he would step up and
work at making them both happy.

Suddenly he was enveloped in slim, strong
arms and those enticing lips were kissing a
trail up his chest where his shirt made a vee
at his throat. 'Sounds like a plan to me.'

'A good one?' He grinned through the desire flooding him.

Her answer was to kiss him. A long, deep,
hot-as-hell kiss that sent desire speeding to
his extremities and all places in between.
He could feel her damp swimsuit against
his arm, her cool skin warming where they
touched, and he wanted her. So much he was
going to explode if they stayed here any longer. 'Sorry, Willow, but—' He gently set her
aside, while wanting to hold on for ever, and
put the gear in drive then pulled out onto the
road again. 'Forget your clothes. I'm taking
you home where you won't need to be wearing anything.'

Sinking back onto her seat, she laughed;
a deep husky sound that tightened him even
harder. Her hand was on his shorts, touching
his erection. 'Bring it on.'

'Not if you keep doing that. We won't get
far. I'll prang the ute and then where will we

go?' He pulled her hand away, placed it on his thigh. It was the hardest thing he'd had to do in a long while. But necessary if they were to get to his house. He was busting to take Willow, but out here on the street where kids were walking and skateboarding? Not likely.

'I hate it when you play sensible.' Her laughter was another aphrodisiac. Raspy, deep, sexy.

'So do I.' How could he be this hard and still able to concentrate on getting them safely to his house? His instinct was to plant his foot and speed through the streets. Common sense—how did he still have that?—made him go carefully. Thankfully he lived close to the beach. 'Here we are,' he said as he swung into his drive after what seemed like for ever.

Willow had her door open almost before he pulled on the brake.

'Come on, boys, you need to get out to the back yard now.' He had the back door open, bouncing with impatience as the dogs slowly stood up and wandered towards him. 'Come on, will you? Don't go for slow and careful today.'

They both jumped out and began sniffing their way up the drive.

Willow laughed. 'They're playing with

you.' Then she groaned. 'And me.' Taking the collar of one, she headed for the gate, dog in one hand, crutch in the other. It was a lopsided run but she was getting there. 'Is this where they go?'

Yes.' He was right behind that delectable body, his other pet in hand, ready to catch Willow if she tripped.

As soon as the dogs were through the gate he took her hand and raced around to his front door. It took three attempts to get the key in the lock, but finally they tumbled inside, and he kicked the door shut with his heel before sweeping Willow into his arms and lifting her up against the wall. Her thighs instantly wound around him, her hands gripped his shoulders, and that mouth—hell, her lips were playing havoc with the skin on his neck, the line down his chest.

'Wait,' he groaned. 'We're in this together.'

A hot wet lick across his nipple was her answer.

He nearly dropped her, the shock and heat so demanding.

Pulling the straps of her swimsuit down, he exposed her breasts and returned the compliment, licking and sucking first one nipple then the other, feeling her buck against him, hearing her need in a short, sharp groan. More licking, more sucking. It wasn't enough. His hand pulled at the fabric covering her lower body. 'Need you out of this.'

She shimmied down his body to stand on one foot and tugged the damned swimsuit off that sensational body. 'Ditto.'

Oh, yeah, of course. Clothes. His shorts and shirt hit the floor with unbelievable speed and he was lifting her up against him again, feeling her thighs holding onto him, her hand seeking, finding his erection.

'Here.' He handed her the condom from his pocket, always prepared these days. What was more, Willow got a thrill putting them over him.

She was wet and hot and quivering.

He pushed into that inviting depth, pulled back, entered her again, and again, and she cried out, her head tipped back, her hands bringing him to a peak, and then he was joining her, coming with her, as one.

Guess that was a real make-up, Willow thought as she stretched out beside Carter on his bed. Not that they'd broken up, because they weren't a couple. Not quite. Though it was feeling more and more as if they might be. First Axel had got to her and now Carter.

Thinking of Axel… 'Hope the dogs are all right.'

'They'll be fine. They're in their yard, can't get out, plenty of shade and water. What more could they want?'

'I think they were a little shocked at being hustled out of the ute so fast.' Did that mean no other woman had stirred him up as much?

'Can't say it's happened before,' Carter told her with a gleam in his eye. 'You are such a distraction it's crazy.'

'Good.' She'd take compliments any day.

'Damn. My phone's still in the truck. I'm half expecting a call from my brother about a bull that's not well.' He was off the bed and heading down the hall. 'I can't believe I forgot it. Actually, I can. You really got to me.'

'Hope you're going to put on some shorts before you head out to your ute.' His clothes were on the floor out by the front door. She didn't do sharing and if any female saw that stunning sight she might be in for a contest.

'Why?' he called back.

She laughed and sat up. They'd come in here after that amazing sex to spread out on the bed and get their breath back. What still got to her and warmed her heart was how Carter barely noticed she was missing a leg.

It made her feel special. He treated her how she wanted to be—normal.

Now she'd like to go sit on the deck. She needed some clothes to do that and they were in the ute too. Her swimsuit was a damp bundle on the floor by the front door and not a lot of use. Hopefully Carter would realise. Getting off the bed, she hopped out of the room, ruing the fact she couldn't walk normally. Sometimes, like now, it hurt not to be able to stroll along as other people did. Hopping around like this only underlined her disability and when Carter came back inside he would notice.

Yes, and he's just made love to you and not blinked or hesitated. Get over yourself.

A huff of air crossed her lips. She was being a sorry puss, which was unlike her. But then Carter was becoming important to her and that made her more aware of her flaws. Was she looking for reasons he might back off? Or reasons she could walk away again? No, she didn't want to do that. He was special, and she wanted more. Had a lot to give too.

The sound of paws on the tiles reached her. 'They sound happy.'

'They're always happy,' Carter told her as he handed over her shirt and shorts. 'In case you want to lounge on the deck.' He grinned. 'Though I'm happy if you don't cover up that sexy body.' He then handed her the prosthesis she'd left at home while going swimming. 'Lena gave me this when I said I was hoping to pick you up.

He still didn't glance at her stump. Hadn't once, and it hadn't been in an 'I mustn't look' way. He was relaxed with her, accepted her as she was. It was time to get over her hang-ups and appreciate how he treated her. 'Thanks. I was hoping you'd bring them in.'

'Help yourself to a shower if you want. I'll open up the house and put the barbecue on. You hungry? It's early but I'm starving.'

'Me too.' A shower sounded good. She could get rid of the salt that had dried on her skin and in her hair. 'I'll be out there shortly.' Dressed, though without underwear because she'd had her swimsuit on.

'Take your time. We're not going anywhere.'

So she was here for the evening. Unless that call came from his brother. Maybe all night. That sounded perfect. How had she managed to stay away from him for the last few nights? It seemed crazy now that they'd made love again and were back to getting along so well.

The shower was luxuriant. The only thing that would've made it better was having Carter in there with her. Willow laughed as she dried off. Talk about greedy, but, heck, he was awesome. When he made love, well, phew, he was out of this world. Her skin heated as she thought about how he brought her to the edge.

Loud banging on the front door interrupted her daydreaming. Then shouts. 'Carter, are you in there? Mate, where are you? Milly's been hit by a car.'

'I'm coming,' Carter called.

Who was Milly? A person or someone's pet? Willow joined Carter on his front steps.

'Mate, can you hurry? She's a mess. Blood everywhere and I reckon her leg's broken.'

'I'll get my bag from the ute,' Carter said.

Had to be an animal if he needed his kit. 'I'll get it,' Willow said. 'Tell me where you're going.'

'Jack? Where is she?'

The man was already charging away. 'On the path outside our house,' he called over his shoulder.

'Through the gate on the back fence and around to the front you'll find us,' Carter told her and raced after Jack.

Grabbing her crutch, she went to get the

bag and headed in the direction the men had gone, thankful for the gate as climbing over the fence would've been tricky. The closer she got, the more voices she heard. Someone was crying.

Then she saw an enormous dog lying on the footpath, whimpering in pain, and blood pulsing out of a deep gash in its shoulder. Both front legs looked to be shattered, not a straight line in sight. Her heart lurched. This was not good.

Carter was on his knees beside the dog, which looked to be a Rhodesian ridgeback. He was touching those legs ever so carefully, feeling the bones, trying to ascertain the damage.

She pushed past two girls to place the bag beside him. 'Want a hand?'

'Yes.'

She made her way around to the other side of the dog. It was awkward because of the people hovering, waiting on Carter to give them good news, to say nothing was as bad as it looked. 'Excuse me. I'm a vet nurse and can help.'

It felt like a universal sigh as people moved as little distance as possible to let her through. Finally she got down on her knees and reached out to Milly's throat, feeling for a pulse.

'It's erratic,' Carter told her. 'Shock.'

Opening the bag, she found cotton wads. Pressing one to the gaping wound on the shoulder, she held it in place and pushed hard in an attempt to slow the bleeding while Carter continued checking over the rest of the dog's body.

Then he looked up. 'Jack? We need to get Milly to the clinic.' He dug into the bag, withdrew a syringe and vial of painkiller. 'But first you need this, Milly.'

'I'll get my car.' Jack was gone.

'Willow, can you drive my ute? It's an automatic.'

'Yes.'

'Good. Head away now and open up the clinic. The keys are on the bench.' He sounded terse but she knew he was concerned for the dog's life. 'Prepare the operating room.'

'On my way.'

He didn't answer but then she didn't expect him to. He was focused on Milly and no doubt working through what he had to do once they had the dog on the table.

With keys in hand, Willow quickly locked up the house before heading to the clinic. There she turned on lights, pulled on scrubs, and wiped down the table even though it was spotless. You couldn't be too careful when it came to infections. Milly was going to need all the care she could get. Placing a sterile sheet on the table, she turned to getting all the equipment ready that might be needed.

'Willow?' Carter called from somewhere out front. 'Can you bring out a board?'

'Yes.' She had that ready too. How they'd got a dog as large as Milly into the car without causing any more damage she didn't know. 'It's by the reception desk,' she replied.

'Got it.' Worry deepened his voice. 'You're quick,' he said as he headed outside.

She thought ahead, that was all. Better to have had a board ready in case it was needed than have them turn up and she couldn't find one fast. She followed Carter in case there was something else she might be needed for.

The car was a sedan and Milly was lying on the flat space at the back. At least that was better than having to be laid on the seat. Between them, Carter and Jack lifted her onto the board and brought her inside. A woman hovered beside them all the time.

Willow crossed to her. 'I'm Willow, a nurse here. I'll be helping Carter,' she told her in case she hadn't taken in the fact she was able to help back at the roadside. 'Come inside where you will be more comfortable. There's tea or coffee if you want it.'

'Thank you. I'm so worried.' Tears streamed down her face.

'Of course you are. Trust me, Carter will do everything he can.' She didn't say 'to save Milly'. She didn't have to. This woman understood the seriousness of the situation.

'I know. He's good. I'm Amy, by the way.'

Inside, Willow closed the door behind them and said, 'Try to make yourself comfortable. Jack will be out here in a minute.' He wouldn't be staying in the operating room while they worked on their patient. It would be too distressing, and distracting for Carter.

'Willow, I'm intubating first. Milly needs help breathing,' Carter told her the moment she joined him after seeing Jack out.

Passing him the tube, she took the dog's head and tipped it back to make it easier for Carter to insert the tube. Next she taped the tube in place while he held it as still as possible.

'Right, X-rays.'

She swung the overhead machine around and waited for instructions about where to take the images.

'Head, shoulders, both front legs. Abdomen, lower legs.' He held Milly in different places for each image, those gentle hands, oh, so careful even when she wouldn't be able to feel a thing now that the drugs were taking affect. Worry poured off him.

'You know this dog well?'

'More I know Jack and Amy well. They've been friends since I moved into my house. They're heartbroken about this.'

Willow drew a long breath when the image of the left front leg appeared on the screen. 'Not good.'

Carter stared at the screen. 'I might be able to save it, but is that the best option? Recovery will be long and painful, and frankly I'm not sure it's worth it. Those bones will never be strong again. She'd be better off with a prosthesis.'

'Time to talk to mum and dad.'

'Yep. I'll be back.'

Willow shifted the X-ray machine out of the way, cleaned up the table around Milly, and kept an eye on her vital signs. She was doing well despite the seriousness of her injuries. There being no internal bleeding or damage to organs helped. But broken bones were no picnic and the shock would take its toll too.

'We're going for amputation,' Carter announced when he strode back into the room twenty minutes later. 'The other front leg has a fracture that will heal given time. We'll suture the shoulder first in case of more bleeding.' He stopped by the table, staring down at the dog. 'Gees, Milly, why did you chase that cat out onto the road?'

'That's what happened? I'm surprised a cat would hassle a dog as large as Milly.'

'So am I. Especially since Milly is usually very placid.' Carter snapped on gloves. 'Right, here we go.' Then he paused, looked at Willow. 'Not quite how we expected the rest of the afternoon to pan out, is it?'

'It is what it is. And, Carter...' She smiled. 'Other than Milly being injured and her owners worried sick, I wouldn't have it any other way. This is us.' Saying that felt like a weight lifting from her heart. She was ready to go forward, to have a relationship with Carter, to find out if she could let go the past and make the most of the future.

'You're right.' His eyes locked with hers for a moment, intent and caring—and surprised. 'It's good. We're good.'

Carter straightened up and stepped back from the operating table, used his wrist to wipe his brow. 'Thank goodness that's over.'

Willow nodded as she lightly touched Milly's head. 'You can say that again.'

'Thank goodness that's over.' Dang, his back ached from leaning over the table for so long.

She chuckled, then her smile slipped. 'Now the hard times really start for Milly.'

'True. I'd better phone Jack and let him know Milly's come through okay.' The couple had gone home after making the decision on how Carter was to proceed with Milly. It had been hard seeing his mate swiping tears away when he thought no one was looking. Jack was one tough dude except when it came to Amy and his dog. 'They'll be sitting with their phone, waiting for this.'

'You're giving them better news than they were expecting when Milly was brought in.' Wise Willow to the fore. She was the best support person for him. She understood how he hurt when his patients and their owners hurt. So did other people, but somehow Willow made it easier for him to do what he had to.

'Be back shortly.'

'Don't rush. I'm not going anywhere.' Once more she was tidying up around Milly, and regularly touching the dog with her fingers.

'Good.' He knew how soft and comforting

her touch was. Yeah, and how hot and sexy her touch could be when they were getting horny. Was it only three hours ago they'd been having it off up against his hallway wall? How things could change so drastically in an instant. From insanely wonderful to sadly worrisome.

But it was his job to put animals back together, and his need to have a woman who tipped him off centre with only a look. The need was new. Or was it? Had he been hiding it for so long he didn't recognise what was holding him back until along came Willow Taylor? She'd changed him in ways he hadn't thought possible. He could admit to wanting love again. Not sure he was ready to step up and take it on yet, but, hell, he was close. So close he could feel his heart lighten with anticipation. So near that every morning when he woke up the day beckoned.

'Carter?' Willow placed a hand on his shoulder. 'You all right?'

Yes. No. Maybe. No, damn it, he was better than all right. Leaning in, he kissed her lightly, not needing to show her the intensity of his feelings, only wanting to caress her lips as a way of saying thank you for turning up in his life. 'I'm fine.'

'Then get on with phoning your friends. They'll be beside themselves with worry.'

While I'm thinking about you and where you might be taking me.

'On to it.' What else could he say? He wasn't ready to tell her how he felt. Not quite. As he left the room he hit Jack's number.

'Carter? Is Milly okay?'

'She's doing well, Jack. She's sleeping, with plenty of painkillers on board. I'm also giving her strong antibiotics to prevent infection.'

'Will she really recover?' Amy asked.

So they were on speaker phone. Fair enough. 'Like I said when you had to make the decision about amputation, it is going to be a stressful few weeks until the fractured leg mends. Lots of TLC and not a lot of moving around required. The stump will heal more quickly but the residual pain will go on longer, may never go away completely, but we can deal with that as it occurs.'

'You're saying she's going to survive, aren't you?' Jack again.

'Yes, Jack, Amy, I am. But we have to remain vigilant about infection. More about that when you take her home. I'm keeping her here for a few days. I know you want her at home as soon as possible, but we need to change dressings and check her wounds regularly.'

'Do what you have to, mate. She's our baby. You know that. Can we visit?'

'Of course you can.' He stepped back into the room where Milly lay on the table, oblivious to everything. 'Right now she's sound asleep, and Willow's keeping her company.' They made a gorgeous pair. Willow definitely needed a dog in her life.

She glanced at him and shook her head, as if she knew what he was thinking.

'Tell her thanks from us.'

He'd be telling her more than that as soon as he got off the phone, but he suspected that'd be a while yet. His friends were needing support and probably had a load of questions for him.

'Coffee?' Willow mouthed.

He nodded, a long breath slipping across his lips. 'Please,' he said.

He finished the coffee at the same time as Jack finally hung up. 'I almost don't want to go home in case they come over the fence with more questions.'

'We can stay here for a while. I'll order in some food.'

At the mention of food his stomach growled.

'Good idea. Double helpings of everything. I'm beyond starving now.'

Willow gasped. 'You didn't get around to turning the barbecue on, did you?'

'No. I was going to get my phone when all hell broke loose.'

'That's a relief.' Willow shuffle-hopped around the table.

'How're you feeling? You've been without your prosthesis throughout the whole time.' He hadn't even thought about it. What did that make him?

'Relax. I'm good. No prosthesis, no pain. Hopping comes naturally nowadays. I wasn't stopping to get it when you needed me here fast.'

'You've put on clean scrubs.'

'No underwear.' She grinned. 'Really getting back to basics, aren't I?'

'If it helps, I like you at basic levels. I'd prefer no scrubs though.' Her nipples would be obvious and her breasts would move gently as she went about looking after Milly or tidying up.

'Order in some food and keep your mind above my neck.' She laughed. 'What's the plan for the night? You'll want to keep a close eye on Milly for a while.'

'I'll stay here for the next couple of hours and then come back a couple of times throughout the night.' He'd take her home except she was large and moving her wouldn't be easy or comfortable. She was better off in a cage—which they still had to get her into. 'First I'll go next door to the liquor outlet and ask one of the guys to give me a hand to shift her.' No way was Willow helping when she didn't have her prosthesis to balance on.

'The sooner the better,' Willow agreed. 'She's starting to move a bit in her sleep.'

When they finally had the dog settled and the takeaways ordered to be delivered, Carter went to the fridge and grabbed two beers. 'Let's sit out in the yard and unwind.'

'Best idea you've had since the one where you turned the ute around and we raced to your house.'

'So beer and pizzas are as good as sex?'

'Right this moment they are. I'm ravenous. Too much exercise and too little food.' She sipped from the bottle and faked a shiver. 'That's so good.'

'I'll have to fix your appetite, one of them, so as I can work on the other later.'

'You think you're going to have time? Seems you've already got a busy night ahead.'

'Never too busy to make love to a sexy woman named Willow.'

'The first time I met you I thought you were a man of few words. Now I'm not so sure. Sometimes there's no guessing what you'll come out with.' She got all thoughtful. 'You were like that from the moment you went to Milly's aid on the street, only said what was necessary. Very focused.'

'Only way to be in emergencies. Saves errors and misunderstandings.' And kept his worries under control.

'Focused, and other times, impulsive. You're not a Gemini by any chance?'

'You're not going to read my stars and tell me what's going to happen in the coming weeks?' he joked.

'Not a hope. Just trying to find out when your birthday might be.'

'June.' She wouldn't be here for it. Unless— Unless they got on so well he could convince her to stay. Was he that ready to see where this went? He might be. Make that, yes, he was. What if it went all wrong? What if he couldn't talk her into staying? To move in with him so they could get to know each other on every level? His heart would be broken. Again. Well and truly. There'd never be a third chance. He wouldn't be able to deal with that.

You're getting ahead of yourself, Carter. You're sharing a beer, going to have pizzas together. Stop with the deep stuff, focus on the here and now and enjoy it.

'So I was right. You're a Gemini.'

'What are you?'

'Aquarius. January twentieth.'

'Your birthday was the week before you started working here.'

'You're on to it. I went home for a night to see Mum and Dad and to have a birthday dinner.'

'Can I ask?'

'Twenty-nine.'

'So a big one next year.' He turned thirty this year and intended having a party to celebrate. All family and friends invited. 'It's mine this year. Want to come to the celebrations?'

She didn't even hesitate. 'I'd love to. As long as I'm not too far away,' she added almost as an afterthought.

Knock him down. 'You're sure?'

'Yes.' Straightening her back, she locked eyes with him. 'I might be in New Zealand by then but it's not a long flight back to Brisbane.'

'You'd do that just to come to my birthday?'

'Not *just* to come, but to *celebrate* with you.'

'You're a marvel.' Hauling her into his arms, he kissed her. 'Did I mention your kisses are something else?'

Ding dong.

'Guess that's dinner.' Willow pulled out of his arms. 'I'll get it.'

'No, you won't. This one's on me.' He headed inside, not giving her a chance to argue. He wanted to do this, to give her anything she wanted. No big deal over who paid for the pizzas, but it was one way of showing Willow he cared about her. A little way, but he hoped one of many to come.

CHAPTER SEVEN

'THE WEATHER'S PERFECT for a wedding,' Willow said as Carter held the taxi door open for her outside the venue where Pip and Billy were going to exchange their vows. They were in Brisbane, staying at a hotel for the weekend to save the nearly one-hour drive after the wedding. Carter looked stunning in his dark grey suit and white shirt with a red tie. 'How did you know I would be wearing red?'

'I saw the shoes when you were showing Kathy.'

She glanced down at her impulse buy. As close to impulse as it could get when buying shoes was often a nightmare. The days of high heels were over. Too awkward. But these shoes were snazzy and cut stylish low and with a small heel. 'I love them.'

'They're a good match to your dress, which

is smashing, by the way. You look beautiful,' he said with a catch in his voice.

No wonder she felt so drawn to Carter. He said the most wonderful things. Her dress fell just below her knees. She'd made a decision not to cover up her prosthesis, preferring to be fashionable than out of date *and* on low heels. Carter added to her confidence by never criticising her for exposing her deformity. Slipping her arm through his, she said, 'You make me feel good.'

'It's not exactly hard.' He kissed her cheek. 'Let's go join in the fun.'

'Let's.' They strolled in, Willow grateful for Carter being with her. Lately everything seemed to come back to this wonderful guy who had her smiling more than normal, feeling happier and hopeful for more.

'Where do you want to sit?' he asked.

'Towards the back.'

'No, you don't, Willow,' said a familiar voice behind her. 'You're up the front with the rest of Pip's friends.'

Turning around, she said to Pip's mother, 'You're supposed to be taking the day off from organising everything.' Leaning in, she hugged Faye. 'How are you doing?'

'Nervous as all be, and really excited.' Faye glanced at Carter and her smile tightened. 'So this is your date.' Nothing like her son, Dave, for which Willow was grateful.

'Carter, I'd like you to meet Faye Greenslade, Pip's mum. Faye, this is Carter Adams.'

'Hello, Faye. Thank you for allowing me to be here with Willow. Though I'm not sure if she forewarned you.' He smiled.

'She did. Though—'

Willow cut her off before she could say something that might make Carter uncomfortable, like the fact she'd prefer Willow were here with Dave. 'We'll go sit down while you greet some more guests.' And get away from trouble.

Faye nodded. 'Fair enough.' She knew exactly what Willow was doing. She'd been trying to set Dave up with Willow on and off over the last few months.

As they made their way closer to the front and sat down Willow smiled and waved to the few people she knew, including Billy, who was standing at the front with his groomsmen looking both excited and nervous. 'Billy and Pip met only ten months ago. They'd have got married within the first weeks if they could've arranged the wedding faster.'

'Why look so nervous?'

'I think Billy is scared he's going to wake

up and find this is all a dream.' She laughed. 'He's just perfect for Pip. And she for him.'

'Lucky them,' Carter muttered more to himself than her.

She glanced sideways, saw colour creep into his face. Like he might be a little envious. 'Hey, hang in there. You never know what's around the corner.' It was true. Perhaps she should listen to herself and take a chance on finding love—with Carter. He was everything she envisaged in any close, strong relationship she'd be a part of. She had accepted his invitation to his birthday party because she couldn't say no. She wondered about that. She did want to go to it, but it frightened her to think she'd actually agreed to come back especially. That showed how much he was coming to mean to her, and she still didn't know if she was ready to make such a commitment.

The music changed, and everyone stood, looking back down the aisle to the bride beside her father.

Willow blinked as she stared at her friend strolling along, clinging to her father's arm, beaming as she stared ahead to Billy, eyes for no one else.

Willow reached for Carter's hand, held tight as she swallowed. Pip looked beautiful in a cream gown that flowed behind her, but it was the love radiating from her eyes that really twisted Willow's gut. Love. It was beautiful. Powerful. She wanted it. But it could cost so much.

'Here.' Carter passed her a folded handkerchief from his trouser pocket.

She didn't know men carried those any more. As she carefully blotted her cheeks, wary of smudging her make-up, she looked at him again, taking in his tall frame and how wonderful he looked all scrubbed up in that stylish suit. Her kind of man—if she had a kind. Mostly she'd avoided thinking about who could fill her heart and have her back in any crisis. Now it seemed she'd found out anyway. Could she give back as much?

Carter took the handkerchief and stuffed it in his pocket, then took her hand again. He didn't have to say a word. He had her back when she got all emotional without making any drama out of it.

She was happy. She was with the right man. Settling nearer to him, she watched the celebration unfold.

'Pippa Greenslade, will you take this man to be your lawful husband?' the marriage celebrant asked.

'I will. I do. I love you, Billy.'

'Billy Ross, will you take this woman to be your lawful wife?'

'Absolutely. Try stopping me.'

Laughter broke out amongst the guests and Billy used the moment to give Pip a quick kiss.

Willow's heart tightened. Pip and Billy were so in love it was wonderful. They looked perfect together.

Carter returned the handkerchief to her. 'Here.'

She hadn't realised she was crying. Not one or two tears this time either. A blush reddened her cheeks as she dabbed carefully. When she glanced sideways she met Carter's gaze.

He was smiling so softly it made her cry more.

'I now declare you married,' said the celebrant loud and clearly.

Everyone began clapping. Willow used the moment to finish drying her face and tuck the handkerchief into her clutch bag. No point giving it back to Carter when she might need it again. Who'd have thought she'd be so moved by the simple, loving moments? Something like envy touched her. This was what she'd been avoiding and here she was feeling as if she might be wrong. It wasn't that she didn't want to love and be loved, she reminded herself. It was the consequences if it went wrong or something dreadful happened that kept her rigid about her feelings.

A firm hand on her elbow indicated she should stand up as the bride and groom were making their way down the flower-strewn aisle. Glad one of them was on the ball, she smiled. Left to her own resources she'd probably be sitting on her chair while everyone else moved out to the marquee that was set up overlooking the Brisbane River.

Pulling her shoulders back, she stood tall and straight, breathed deep, and met Dave's direct stare as he followed the bridal party. A little smile lifted her mouth. 'Hello, Dave.'

'Willow.' He nodded. Then his gaze slid to Carter and his mouth tightened.

Yep, I'm with an amazing man who seems to like me for myself.

Dave moved on and it was their turn to move out to the marquee. Slipping her hand in Carter's, she tugged lightly. 'Let's join the fun.'

'I don't think I've witnessed such a moving ceremony,' he said as they followed everyone outside.

He'd felt it too? Said a lot about him. 'Me either. Pip is so happy.'

'I'd say the same for Billy.' Carter laughed. 'Exactly how they should be on their wedding day.' Then his laugh stopped abruptly and a shadow crossed his face.

Grabbing his arm, Willow pulled him to the side and away from the crowd, before wrapping him in a hug. That reaction had been right from his heart. He was thinking about his own wedding day. Unable to think of anything to say that might help, she just held him, and hoped those awful memories wouldn't stay with him all day. He deserved better.

Talk about making a fool of myself, Carter thought. *Willow will think I'm still so tied up in the past that there isn't anything left for her.* She was hugging him. Leaning back, he looked down at the lovely woman holding him tight. 'I'm fine.' He was, actually. Apart from a brief moment when an old dream had flashed in his head, he was happy. Whatever he and Cass had thought they had planned, it didn't eventuate and there was no going back. He was here with Willow, in the present, not the past.

'Good, though I'll use any reason to hug you.' Her grin tickled him, made him happier than ever to be with her.

'Come on. We might be missing out on the fun.' He took her hand as they walked towards the marquee. 'What's happening next?'

'Photos while we all enjoy champagne. What could be better?'

A lot of activities sprang to mind. He forced them aside and picked up two glasses of bubbles from a passing waiter. 'To a lovely couple,' he said. He was not thinking of Willow and himself. Not much.

There was a wicked twinkle in Willow's eyes as she linked her arm through his and tapped her glass against his. 'To a lovely couple,' she repeated, and took a sip. The same thoughts tripping through her head?

For someone who'd been averse to weddings since his hadn't happened, by the time the band began to play and people got up to dance after the dinner, Carter had to admit this was a great one. Everyone was friendly, the atmosphere was buzzing, the happy couple smiling non-stop, and the speeches had Willow digging for his handkerchief more than once. 'You've surprised me today,' he said.

'You didn't think I could cry?' she said as she mopped at the corners of her eyes. 'When it's so romantic?'

So that was what was in the air. Romance. Of course it was, and he'd been trying to ignore it, even when Willow sat so close their shoulders and thighs touched. The air between *them* was electric. And romantic? Could be. He wasn't looking too hard. That moment when he'd remembered his wedding day had shown him he wasn't ready for a steady relationship. Not even with Willow. He couldn't deny he'd accepted her hug and hadn't wanted to let her go though. Which said he wasn't completely against getting closer. In fact he was fooling himself if he thought that.

'I've never seen you so emotional. Nor so happy.'

'Do you want to dance?' Willow surprised him.

Though why was he surprised? She didn't hold back from anything that he'd seen. 'Let's.' He stood up and held her chair.

She bounced out onto the dance floor and turned to him, winced when her bung leg was slow to follow her. 'Show me your moves, man.'

'Are you ready for this?' If she expected him to bop around as though he didn't have any moves she was mistaken. Taking her hand, and placing his hand on her waist, he began to dance them around the floor, dodging other people, moving in time.

Willow grew tense as she limped. 'Dammit.'

He kept dancing, holding her close but not so near to get in the way of that prosthesis. 'Don't hesitate. Keep moving to the music. I'm right here with you.'

'You're good at this,' Willow told him when he kept her from tripping.

'Never know when I might have to dance out of the way of an angry bull.'

The back of her hand touched his neck, rubbed softly. 'This is wonderful.'

'It is.' His chin tucked onto the top of her head as he pulled her closer. 'Just relax and follow me.'

When the band took a short break, Willow gripped his hand and headed back to their table where she downed a small glass of water, her eyes alight with wonder and fun. 'I've never enjoyed dancing so much.'

His chest puffed out like a proud adolescent. 'Then you'll want to get back out there shortly.'

'Maybe.' She looked around the room. 'Or we could sneak away early.'

'We can do both.' A bit more dancing wouldn't hurt. Holding Willow close and feeling her body move to the music was as sexy as any move she'd made with him so far. 'That hotel bed isn't going anywhere.' It would get a workout later. 'Want some more champagne?' She'd only had two all evening, and he knew she enjoyed it.

'I'd love one.'

'I'll be back.' He headed across to the bar.

'Carter, I hope you're enjoying yourself.' The bride's mother had turned from talking to a couple as he waited for his order. 'Willow seems happy.'

Why wouldn't she be? 'It's been a wonderful wedding, thank you.'

'The perfect couple, aren't they?' Faye glanced over to her daughter and son-in-law, who were chatting to a group of friends. 'They'll go far in life.'

Sounded more like a business arrangement when she put it like that. 'It's obvious they're very much in love.'

'It isn't the love that'll take them the whole distance. It's everything else they have that'll buy the house, educate the children, give them comfort on the bleak days.'

Then he'd got everything wrong and should've married the woman from a wealthy family he'd met at vet school. They'd liked each other enough to have the occasional coffee or meal together, but not enough to kiss or go further. But she did have a bank account worth a small fortune. Which, while making life comfortable, to use Faye's words, would not have made his heart soar. Something he believed was there with Pip and Billy.

'You don't seem to agree with me,' Pip's mother said.

'Your champagne, sir.' The barman placed two full, sparkly glasses in front of him.

Saved by the wine pourer. 'Thank you.' Picking the glasses up, he nodded to Faye and stepped away, felt her watching him as he returned to Willow. Willow. *She* could make his heart soar if he wasn't careful. Damn it, it was already in the air.

'Faye give you grief?' Willow asked as he sat down.

She didn't miss a thing. 'Not really, but I got the feeling she would've preferred you'd come with someone else.'

'She's mentioned on more than one occasion that I'd be missing out on so much not coming with her son, Dave. I don't understand. I'm not his type. Faye might be getting desperate that he's not going to settle down soon. She's driven by a need to see her children married and having babies. She gave Pip a lot of grief over her lack of attention to finding the right man, which only made Pip more determined to get her career under way and have ticked off some boxes about travel before she fell in love.'

'How did that go?'

'Being Pip, it went according to plan. Except I don't think she ever envisaged falling so much in love that none of her plans mattered half as much as being with Billy.'

'I can't imagine planning to find love. It doesn't work like that. Not for me.' Although it had been a bit that way with Cassandra. They got along as kids, talked about always being together when they were teenagers, and then continued along the path of their dreams for careers and marriage and family. There hadn't been a lot of spontaneity, more a moving on with what they'd talked about growing up.

'Stop thinking too much.' Willow was smiling, but behind that she knew what he was thinking.

'How do you do that?'

'What?'

'Know what's going on in my head? It's a worry. I can't think about anything personal around you.' He laughed. Was he worried? Surprising, but no, not really.

'Yes, you can. How else will I find out what you want? Or need?' Her smile was turning serious. Too serious.

'You'll have to wait until I tell you.' That wouldn't be until he was one hundred per cent certain he knew the answers himself. 'In the meantime, let's have some more fun.'

'Hey, Willow, Carter. You two looked good on the dance floor.' Pip reached down to hug her friend. 'You seriously did,' she said a little quieter. 'He's cool.'

Not so quiet that Carter didn't hear. But he'd pretend otherwise, or it could get awkward if that blush going on in Willow's face was an indicator of discomfort. He stood up and shook Billy's hand. 'Congratulations again. This has to be the best wedding I've ever been to.'

Pip drew back and looked from him to Willow. 'Really? Why? I mean, for us it is definitely the best, but that's because it's ours and we're so in love.' Her hand found her husband's and she brushed a kiss on his knuckles. 'Eh, babe?'

'I'm not arguing.' Billy grinned.

Willow stood up and leaned into Carter. 'It's the love firing between you two that sets this wedding apart. It's been sparking off you both all the time. You've hardly noticed anyone else, as you shouldn't, but that's not always the way of it. Honestly, today's been all about love. That's so special.'

Exactly. He couldn't have said it any better. Carter placed his arm around her waist and held her closer. If ever there was an example of a wedding he'd like to have for himself, then this one was it. A ripple of longing touched his heart, his head. Yes, he really would, and that was a new thought. One he hadn't had since Cass. Maybe not even then because their wedding would've been a continuation of what they'd known most of their lives. 'Well said.'

Pip's permanent smile grew. 'Thanks, guys. And, Carter, I'm glad you came with Willow. She's looking awesome and having a great time. She's enjoying herself.'

At least one of the family was pleased with him, then. Not that it mattered. This wasn't Willow's family. Her parents and brother were the ones he'd have to impress if they went further with their relationship. 'She's thrilled for you.'

Willow nudged him and grinned at her friends. 'She—' she tapped her breast '—has full hearing. She is so happy for you two, and for being here to share this occasion.' Turning slightly his way, she added in a quieter voice, 'And because you're with me.'

Pip tugged her away from his arms and hugged her tight, beating him to it. The bride said something in Willow's ear that caused a small flush of colour in her cheeks. Pulling back, Pip winked at Willow and turned to Billy. 'Is it time to go yet?'

'I was ready the moment you said I do.' Billy laughed. 'Let's have one more dance and then we can say our goodbyes and get the hell out of here and go to our hotel.'

'One more dance,' Willow said to Carter as her friends wandered onto the dance floor as the band started up again. 'Then you and I can get the hell out of here and go to our hotel too.'

'The perfect plan.' Taking her hand, he led them onto the dance floor. 'Not the same hotel, is it?'

'Wouldn't have a clue, but it doesn't matter if it is. No one's going to see those two for many hours to come once they leave here.' She fanned her hands across his chest, heating his skin, teasing him with her body pressed against his. 'Hold me closer,' she whispered.

More than happy to oblige, he tightened his arms around her waist. His legs pushed hers as he danced her around the floor, oblivious to all but the music and the delectable woman in his embrace. Yes, this had been a superb wedding. His would be even better if it ever came about. Keep holding Willow, feeling her, wanting her, loving her, and it just might.

'For someone who's not fond of big cities, you've got this one sussed,' Willow said next morning when they were ambling along the riverside hand in hand, a gentle exhaustion pulling at his body.

'Brisbane doesn't feel like a city to me. It's my home town in a big way. I've been coming here since I was a nipper. Everything's familiar, and how I like it.' He was not excitement on steroids when it came to travel. 'Don't ask me why, but I prefer being in smaller towns, or out in the rural landscape. I've always felt like that.'

'Probably part of growing up on the farm. You know that space and feel a freedom that you wouldn't get in a city. Whereas I love the noise and busyness and the hype. In the countryside I keep looking for what's missing.' She paused, and looked over the river.

'I have to admit I didn't feel that out at your parents' place.'

Carter had to strain to hear her. A big admission for her, or a shock? 'Could be that was because the farm's not far from Southport and you knew you could be back in town within a short time.'

'You're making it sound as though I'm paranoid about being out in the open.' She shivered. 'Maybe I am.'

'If you are, then I might be too, for the opposite sensations.'

'We make a good mix, then.' Her smile had returned.

Thank goodness. He missed that beam whenever she withdrew it. 'I think we already knew that, if last night is anything to go by.' They'd made love twice in the enormous bed in their hotel room and ordered room service at two o'clock because they were starving. 'Now I think about it, if this is city living, I could possibly get to love it.'

Her laughter was light and touched him all over. 'Next stop Paris?'

Laughter bubbled up. 'Why not? For a few days at the most.' Very unlikely. Though possibly not when with Willow. Anything seemed possible with her at his side.

'See Paris in a few days? I doubt it. If I

ever get there I'll be staying for weeks, not days.'

'So you haven't been there? Is it on your bucket list?'

She shrugged. 'Of course I'd love to go to Paris, but I tend to go to places where I can work. I was training for a trip to France with a cycling team before the accident, and Paris was part of the itinerary. Since then I haven't given it much thought.'

'See, this is where we are different. If, and that's a big if, I were to travel across the world, I'd want to go to wine-growing regions or coastal villages.'

'I'd want to see those too, along with the cities full of historical buildings and sites, and endless streets of food and music and art. People talking non-stop in languages I don't understand a word of.' Excitement lifted her voice, made her step lighter.

'I wonder if I could shuck off my inertia about sightseeing and do something like what we're talking about.' With Willow?

'Only one way of knowing,' she said quietly.

'Yes, and we're a long way from doing something like that together.' He was falling deeper and deeper in love with her, but caution still ruled. Not as strong, but it was there. Yesterday's wedding had made him sit up and wonder if he could ever have that for himself with the ideal woman, and he'd turned to Willow for a sense of acknowledgement to his heart. But. Wasn't there always one of those? The closer he got to her, the further away the possibility to actually step up and do something about it got. She hadn't made any promises about changing her mind and staying on after her contract with the vet clinic finished.

She's coming to your birthday.

So she had said, and he believed she had meant it at the time, but who knew where she'd be working by then? Even if she did fly in for the party, she'd fly out again within a couple of days. It was who she was, a woman eaten up by her past and unable to stop running from it. Did that sound familiar? He might be grounded in this region, but he wasn't moving on from his own pain either.

Willow jabbed him with an elbow. 'Have I scared you off?'

A little. She had reminded him of the fact these were early days. He didn't believe in falling in love instantly and then everything would turn out fine. He'd only known the long and slow approach, and while his heart seemed to be falling for Willow, his head remained on the fence. Slowing things down a bit might be the wise way to go. 'Not entirely.'

'That's better than totally, I suppose.' She was smiling so he didn't believe he'd upset her.

It was hard to know with Willow. She took most aspects of her life seriously, but seemed more relaxed with him than anyone or anything else. What did she think of him? Was she interested in him more than for a short fling? Her warnings about moving on come the end of March were always there. He'd have to go easy on letting her into his heart. Except it was too late. He already loved her. Not enough to risk dreaming up ideas of living together, or talking about the future, but he could think more about the idea of travelling somewhere exciting with her.

'Have you done a boat trip up the river?' he asked, as much to distract himself as something interesting to do. Not that the Brisbane River held any surprises for him. Growing up in the region, he'd seen it in flood, seen it crowded with boats on occasions when the whole city seemed to come out to celebrate one thing or another. But it would be fun to take Willow up to the trees where hundreds of bats hung out, sleeping through the day and making a permanent mess below.

'I haven't got around to it yet. Are you suggesting we go now?'

'How about it? Then we can get off and have lunch on the way back, before heading back to Southport.' He was so unused to spending a whole weekend with a woman he almost felt awkward. But he wasn't faltering. He wanted to spend as much time as possible with Willow, so he had to be decisive.

Willow swung their hands between them. 'Sounds perfect.'

Didn't it?

CHAPTER EIGHT

'HOW DID THE wedding go?' Willow's flatmate asked on Sunday night.

Almost too well. It had her constantly
thinking about her own future. 'It was beautiful. Pip and Billy looked so in love they
made everyone cry.'

'And Carter? How was he?' asked Lena.

'He didn't shed a tear, but I saw him swallowing hard a couple of times.' He had to
have been thinking about his wedding that
didn't eventuate, but she wondered if there'd
been some thoughts about his future mixed
in there too.

'An emotional man, eh? Can't go wrong
with that as long as he's not over the top
about it.'

Hot, loving, perfect. 'Great. We had a good
time. The man can dance, believe me.' She
could still feel his arm on her waist, her hand
in his as he led her around the floor in per-

fect time to the music. He had other moves that turned her on too.

'You getting used to having him around?'

'I like being with him, but that's as far as it goes.' She wasn't admitting to maybe wanting more. Did she want Carter thinking about them as a couple? It would mean she'd have to make some decisions of her own. To stay or to go? She'd be going. This time would be the hardest yet, but she'd do it. The difficulty came because she cared a lot for Carter and so knew she'd be letting a chance go by, and possibly hurting him.

The image of Pip and Billy looking at each other as though no one else existed and with so much love stirred her big time. It had been beautiful and caught her heart and squeezed it hard. That was what she wanted. More than anything. Enough to stop moving on? A shiver rattled her. Not likely.

'You over-thinking things by any chance?' Lena again.

'Me? Not a chance.'

'You're not fooling me.' Lena picked up the TV remote. 'If you ever want to talk, buy me a wine and I'll be all ears for as long as you like.'

She might've made it sound like a joke, but Willow understood she was serious. It'd been a while since she'd had a friend like that. So much was coming together here. 'Your rates are quite high but I'll remember your offer.'

She'd love to talk, to put out there her feelings for Carter and how confused she was about accepting him into her life more permanently or carrying on doing what she always did—moving away. Running away? She winced. Could be, but it'd worked so far. She hadn't felt like this about a man since Gavin. After how he'd treated her, she hadn't thought she'd be able to fall in love again. Love? She loved Carter? No, it wasn't possible. Or was it?

If that was the case, then she'd let herself in for the biggest let-down yet. 'What am I going to do?'

'Try a new approach to life.'

'Watch your programme.'

'Think about what I said.'

She was. That was the problem. A new approach was tempting if not downright frightening. She could not face losing someone special again. Heading down to her bedroom, she opened up her computer and began looking for jobs in New Zealand. There was little more than a month left on her contract here, but it was never too soon to get the next job sorted. Except when vet clinics needed a nurse they were usually required within a couple of weeks. But there was no harm in looking.

Her chest felt heavy as she clicked through the options. Three positions in Auckland, two in Christchurch and five in other smaller cities across the country. The one she'd seen a few weeks back in Napier had gone. But it was a good result so far. Although most of them were for a nurse to start immediately or within a fortnight, it did show there probably wouldn't be a problem finding employment. One ad was from a new clinic opening in central Auckland wanting to take on three nurses, one to start immediately and the others a little further down the track. Perfect. Auckland was her first pick. A big city to get lost in, have fun, and getting out to see other places would be easy with the transport system. So where was the buzz that usually filled her when she began planning her next stop?

Ignoring the sudden chill lifting her skin, she began filling in the online form, taking her time in the hope the excitement would start to kick in. By the time she'd finished and had attached her CV the chill had died down but her heart was heavy. Was she doing the right thing? Of course she was. This was normal. To be falling at the post because she'd met a man who made her feel whole again was undermining her resilience. Bottom line—she did not want to be hurt. Losing her friends had been dreadful, but it had given her a new strength to use to keep going. But if it were to happen again, whether by death or a broken heart, well, she doubted she'd be as strong a second time.

Send.

See? That was how she did things. Forget the procrastination. Get on with living a life of new thrills every week. Forget wondering about settling down permanently with someone she could love for ever. It was too risky.

Monday and another day working with Carter. Willow drove slowly, as though she could put off the inevitable. During the long hours overnight she'd come to the unhappy conclusion that she'd have to withdraw from seeing him outside work. Three weeks dating and she felt as though her world had changed, so what would it be like to pack up and go if they kept their fling going until she left town?

'Morning, Willow,' Kathy chirped as soon as she walked into the clinic. 'How was the wedding?'

'Truly lovely. Pip looked gorgeous.' And so in love it seemed impossible.

'Carter said something similar.' Kathy followed her out to the staffroom. 'He's switched with Joe this week and will be dealing with the rural jobs, by the way. Though you probably already know that.'

She hadn't had a clue. 'So I'm on with Joe or Seamus this morning?'

'Seamus. Spaying cats seems to be the theme of the morning. Four of them, plus two dogs with hernias.'

'That'll keep me out of mischief.' Willow shut her locker and headed for the coffee she could smell. Why did Carter swap? Had he come to his senses after their weekend? They'd been close all the time, as in happy, sharing, laughing close. Their lovemaking had been phenomenal, but it was all the rest that really got to her and flipped her heart and head.

'Carter will be back in the clinic come Thursday,' Kathy said over her shoulder as she took a mug of coffee out to the front desk.

What was she saying? That Carter had deliberately swapped out so he could avoid her? When they'd had such a fantastic weekend together? Had he got cold feet? The wedding had shaken her, opened her eyes to what she wanted. It had also underlined that getting that could cost dearly, and the old fear had risen fast. There was no way she'd feel hurt by Carter working away from the clinic, because she totally got his reasons. Unless she was reading too much into it and he just needed to do some outdoor work for a change, since he'd done more in the clinic than the other two vets since she'd started here. She probably needed to sit down and talk with him.

She shivered. That'd be too intense when they both understood she wasn't here for long. Within weeks she'd be on a big tin bird out of the country. If she got any positive results to last night's job applications, that was. Knowing it was unlikely to have any replies one way or the other this soon, she still pulled her phone from her pocket and checked her emails. Nothing. A strange sense of relief niggled. Didn't she want to leave Queensland? Leaving Carter was going to be a wrench, but staying here might be an even bigger one if he stuck with the fling that was meant to end soon.

'Morning, Willow.' Seamus sauntered into the room. 'Looks like we've got a list and a half this morning.'

'Spaying being the op of the day, I hear.'

Shoving her phone away, nothing of importance to read, she stood up. 'Want me to get organised?'

'Sit down and finish your coffee.' Seamus squeezed a teabag in a mug of hot water. 'We've got time.'

Sinking back onto her seat, she blew on her coffee and took a sip. 'How was your weekend?'

'Busy. The get together Kathy and I went to started at the Esplanade Restaurant with a fantastic meal like nothing I've experienced before. You been there?'

From what she understood it was a top-range restaurant. When she shook her head, he carried on. 'Give it a go some time. Talk Carter into taking you. The food is excellent, the ambience perfect for couples and the staff non-intrusive.'

Carter take her? When they tended to go to pubs? When they seemed to be taking a breather from each other?

You might be wrong about that, Willow.

'I might take *him*.' She smiled tightly. It would be great to give him a treat for a change.

'He's spending most of the week at his parents' place. Something about checking over the beef herd in between attending the calls that have come in.' Seamus seemed to know she knew nothing about this.

'He was meant to do that a week ago.'

'I know. Too many distractions going on in his life, I reckon.' Seamus grinned. 'You're good for him, Willow. Rattling his cage, I reckon.'

He was rattling hers. 'Glad to hear I'm not alone in the cage.' She laughed, then realised what she'd admitted to Carter's friend. Her smile dropped. 'I'm not here for long though.'

'You're still planning to move on? Abbie's job is still a possibility for you. Last time I talked to her she was saying it's getting less likely she'll return at the end of her leave.'

'I'm thinking of going to New Zealand next.' Not quite answering the question but putting it out there without saying anything about why. 'I've got a couple of applications in at the moment.'

'I see.' Seamus looked disappointed. For Carter? Or for the clinic?

Time to get busy in the operating room. Draining her coffee, she stood up, not about to be held back this time. 'I'll get ready for surgery number one.' Anything to keep her from dwelling on Carter and what it was going to be like leaving here. Did Seamus understand that it didn't change anything if Abbie didn't come back? She *wasn't* staying.

Carter removed the syringe from the bull's hindquarters and stepped back. 'Done.'

'We're about halfway through the herd,' Jock, the farmer, acknowledged as he opened the narrow gate to let the bull out.

At the other end of the blockade a farm hand got ready to let the next animal in.

Preparing the next injection, Carter looked around and breathed in the smell of animals and sunshine. It was good to be outside, away from four walls—and a certain lady stirring up his long-held determination to remain single and safe. What was the point of safe if it meant being lonely and without a family to call his own?

Seeing Willow's friends saying their wedding vows had shocked him into realising how much he did still want that. He'd been wrong to think he could move away from his dreams of love and family, to believe he had achieved it. The longing had been lying in wait, ready to spring to life the moment a wonderful, caring, loving woman came along. In other words, Willow. He should've told her he wouldn't be working in town for the next few days, but it had been a sudden decision and he didn't think he could explain without exposing his feelings for her. And he just wasn't ready for that. His fear of being hurt again seemed to take over whenever he thought he might manage to talk to her about it. Except that had been wrong of him. She deserved better.

Holding his hand up, he said to his client, 'Give me a couple of minutes, will you?' Then he punched Willow's phone number. 'Hi, Willow. How's your week going?' *Mine's feeling a load better already.*

'Busy. How about yours?' Her voice didn't have its light and fun tone, nor was it sad. She wasn't giving anything away, then.

He got straight to the point. 'Willow, I'm sorry for swapping rosters with Seamus but I needed some space. The weekend was so good I had to take a step back and think about some things.' They seemed to meld together and grab at each other physically and mentally. 'I enjoyed every moment spent with you.' There was no doubt about it. He was falling deeper and deeper in love with her. Now three days into the week and he wondered if he'd done the right thing. Three days spent with her lost for ever.

She said nothing.

This was Willow so he waited. Under his ribs a heavy banging was going on.

Nothing.

Should he say something more? Explain himself?

Then he heard her take a breath. 'I understand.'

'You do?' Relief came, quickly followed by concern she might be pleased he'd stepped away.

'Yes. I panicked a bit over how well the weekend went for us too. We get on almost too well it worries me. Then I was disappointed you weren't at work, but it's actually been fine. I was going to call but figured if you needed space then I'd leave you alone.'

The relief grew, outstripped the concern. Once again they'd been on the same page. No wonder they got on so well. 'How about dinner on Friday? I'm staying out here for the whole week but will head back to town Friday afternoon.' *Say yes, you'd love to join me.*

'I'd love that.'

He fist-pumped the air. She'd love to join him.

She wasn't finished. 'I was going to invite you out to a restaurant Seamus recommended, so how about it? My turn to take you out.'

Carter hesitated, then his hand dropped to his waist. It went against the grain to let a woman pay for his evening. But he had to meet Willow halfway on everything or they'd never make it past the starting block. 'Sounds great. What time shall I pick you up?' He was driving, no argument.

'How about six-thirty for a pre-dinner drink?'

Just like that they were back in that same warm happy place they always found together. How had he thought he could step away and not miss her too much? Some things were impossible, and that was up there with the best of them.

Shoving his phone back in his pocket, he gave Jock a nod. 'Next.' Jab, squeeze the syringe, remove the needle, step back. 'Next.'

Another bull was encouraged into the stall by the farmhand's prod.

Jab, squeeze the syringe, remove the needle. 'Next.'

What Willow's feelings for him were, he had no idea. Or was afraid to find out. She seemed keen on him, but that might be him overreacting. They were having a fling, a hot, sexy and loving fling. Did flings usually involve love? That was the component he'd find hard to walk away from when it was over. It would finish. Not once had Willow suggested otherwise. She was leaving Southport, and Queensland, most likely leaving the country when her contract finished. Finished. They'd be finished.

'Next.'

So the big question. Carry on making the most of a wonderful time with an amazing woman or walk away now while some pieces of his heart were still in place? Looking around the yard and paddocks beyond, he knew he had to keep seeing her other than at work. He had to. No argument. No matter the consequences. He was carrying on, eyes wide open. Decision made, he smiled to himself.

Jab, squeeze the syringe, remove the needle, step back.

'Seamus was right. The food is exceptional.' Willow placed her napkin on the table and sat back, a heart-warming smile directed at Carter.

He gave her one back. 'This is where I intended bringing you when I asked you out the other night. Joe and Yvette recommended it months ago, and Seamus followed up on it.

I've been wanting to try this place out for a while, but had to wait until you showed up in my life.' See? When he was with Willow all restraints fell away and he said whatever came to mind without worrying he might be showing too much of himself.

'I beat you to it.' Her laughter tinkled between them. 'What would you like to do now?'

'How about a walk along the beach before heading back to my place?' Where they might make love and cuddle up together for the remainder of the night.

'Best idea I've heard all night.' The wicked glint in her eyes told him she knew exactly what he was thinking.

The weeks of enjoying each other at and outside work flew by. Willow got excited just thinking about going to work after her morning swim at Main Beach. It was nothing to do with the animals and all about Carter. There were animals in need everywhere but there was only one Carter.

Tonight he'd brought her to a nightclub and it was unexpected fun, nightclubs not being her usual haunt. The air was vibrant, the music set her feet tapping, and her blood humming. He meant so much to her now she was starting to panic about leaving. 'So stay,' she muttered as she waited for him to come back to their table.

Stay? Permanently? Settle in one place and make a life for herself? With Carter? Did he want that? Did she?

'Here.' He placed a glass of cold water in front of her. 'Just as you ordered, no ice.'

'Cheers.' It was hot in here.

Carter slid onto the stool beside her, watching the crowd on the dance floor. He looked relaxed and happy. Different from the man she'd first met.

Did she want to stay on? The question gnawed at her. The short answer was, yes. If only she could let go the fear of being hurt again.

Carter wouldn't hurt you. Not deliberately.

She understood that. Just as she wouldn't hurt him either. But what it if didn't work out between them? It might be time to take a chance on life, but whenever she considered doing something about that her blood ran cold with fear.

'What's up?' he asked.

How long had he been watching her? 'Nothing.' She shrugged.

One eyebrow rose pointedly. 'Really?'

She glanced at the dance floor, back at

Carter. He was everything she had ever wished for. Was it enough to hand over her heart? She wasn't ready. When would she be? What would it take for her to decide she could give up running away and stop in one place for ever?

He sighed. 'You're scaring me, Willow.'

She was scaring herself. 'Sorry.' She'd said that a lot lately. Unlike her. Pulling on her game face, she smiled. 'I'm good. Want to dance?'

He looked straight at her, his hand tight around his glass, his foot tapping harder. Finally he answered. 'Yeah, why not?'

She got the feeling it was the last thing he wanted to do, but since they wouldn't be able to talk on the dance floor she stood up and moved in that direction.

His hand took hers as they reached the edge of the heaving crowd, and he pulled her close as she began to shimmy in time to the music. His moves were heavier and less spontaneous. His face was tight, his eyes sad.

Had he read her mind? Did he know the questions circling her mind?

'Hey.' She leaned in and placed a soft kiss on his stubbly chin. 'It's all right.' No, it wasn't but she didn't know what else to say. Especially not when they were here and she'd have to shout to be heard. She didn't have the answers to her doubts either.

Carter held both her hands, watching her move, and slowly he began to move with her, his face softening, the sadness disappearing from his eyes.

She didn't think he'd moved on and would forget those moments, but he was trying to keep the atmosphere between them light and comfortable.

The time to talk was approaching fast, if it wasn't already here. They couldn't carry on as if no big decisions had to be made. Her real problem was that she had no idea if she could take the risk and stay here to try and make a go of their relationship. She didn't know if that was what Carter wanted. He might be glad she'd soon be leaving.

He leaned in. 'Let's head back to Southport and go for a stroll along the beach.'

Her stomach knotted. She'd bet her new shoes they weren't going there to kiss and get all hot with need. 'All right.' But it wasn't. She was suddenly more afraid than she'd been in a long time.

There was a light breeze coming off the sea as they strolled hand in hand along the beach, shoes dangling from their other hands. Carter was cursing himself under his breath. Why had he suggested they walk on the beach where there'd be no interruptions? Willow's expression as she'd sat at that table had told him she was worried about them. He wanted to have it out, clear the air so they could move on happy with their choices. The chances of that were remote. She might like being with him, and getting close, but not once had she hinted she might change her mind about heading away.

'The temperatures are dropping a little now that we're into autumn,' Willow said quietly, as though looking for something to say. Which was new.

And warned him things weren't good for him right now. He followed her premise, suddenly unwilling to open the conversation they needed to have. 'It's still warm enough for swimming and surfing.' The surfers would get the best waves in June, and swimmers would've opted for wetsuits by then. Willow wasn't likely to be around for that. For a moment he felt lonely at the reminder this was a fling, nothing long term. In her book, anyway.

'I've been going out there every day before work. The water temp doesn't feel any different apart from the initial dip. I'm going to miss this.'

'Then don't go.' Carter stopped dead in his tracks, turned to face her. 'I mean it, Willow. Give us a chance.' He had to put it out there. Get this out in the open. Know one way or the other what his future held.

She stared at him. Hope filled her eyes. Her mouth opened, closed again. The hope dimmed. 'I can't. I'm sorry but I'm not ready to stay.'

His shoes landed on the sand as he reached for her shoulders to bring her closer. 'Are you absolutely certain about that?'

'I—' She stopped. Then, 'It's how I cope. I can't take risks. I've had more than enough things go wrong to face anything else.'

It sounded like an excuse, even when it came from her heart. 'We can sort this, work through it together, Willow. Together, as one. Since we met, we've always had each other's backs over problems. Why not this one?'

She turned to look down the beach. Away from him. 'I'm afraid.'

He knew that. So was he. 'Tell me, Willow. I'm here for you, all the way.' She had to open up. It would be good for her. He knew about the crash that tilted her life, but not from her.

Not with her emotions and fears laid out for him to hear and help with.

Slowly she turned back to him and took his hands in hers. She was shaking. 'What about you, Carter? You haven't told me much about what went wrong with Cassandra. I understand you were devastated, but how have you come back from that?'

Fair cop. 'Let's walk while we talk.' Standing still seemed to emphasise their problems, not soften them. As she took a tentative step beside him, he began. 'When you've grown up with the person you fall in love with, you think you know all there is to that person. That's how I felt about Cass anyway. When she turned up two hours before the wedding to call it off, I knew the moment she got out of the car that she was about to blow my life apart. Yet I still hoped I was wrong. How could she when we knew everything there was to know about each other?'

For the first time ever he felt sympathy for Cass and what it must've cost her to tell him she was going away that day. She'd been very brave. He wasn't the only one hurt that day. It would've been so much easier to carry on and pretend all was right in her world.

He continued. 'Therein lay the problem.

We knew each other so well there was no excitement any more. Not that it bothered me. I was happy beyond reason. She was the love of my life. But Cass wanted something else, and I couldn't give it to her.'

They kept walking, and after a while Willow asked, 'Have you ever heard from her since?'

'Not directly. Our parents are still good friends and naturally my folks are up to date on what Cass is doing. They give me the occasional info, but I don't need to know everything. We're finished, and have been for years.' Something he understood more since meeting Willow than he had any time in the past.

'Are you sure you're ready to start over with someone else?'

With you, Willow. With you. 'Yes, I am. But I'll never be certain until I try. That's taking a risk. I understand. But how else do we find new beginnings, find love and have a family?'

'By going slowly?' Her eyes were wide.

'Tell me where you stand, Willow. Do you want to fall in love? To have children?'

'I can't talk about it. The words are stuck in my throat. I can't dislodge them.'

Crunch time had arrived. Carter stopped and turned to look at Willow, his heart's desire. Digging deep, he opened up further. 'I can't trust you if you can't open up to me. I trusted Cass implicitly and she left. I want to believe in you and try again. To give you my heart. But if you want me to wait until you're ready to risk getting close I need something from you. I know you're vulnerable because I recognise it in myself. Talk to me, Willow.'

'I want to, believe me.' She swallowed. Looked away. Returned those sad eyes to him. 'But I can't.'

Taking a step back, he said quietly, 'Then we're at an impasse. I am ready to give you everything, to risk everything, but I need reassurance that you want the same. Then I can be patient until you're ready. But if not—' He ran out of words. Out of hope.

'I'm sorry,' she whispered. Then she turned and began a long, slow walk back the way they'd come.

Back to the road. Back to the loneliness she hadn't admitted to. The same loneliness he'd only realised he was dealing with once he'd met her.

He watched Willow until he couldn't see her any more. Then he turned to walk further along the beach, away from where they'd stood together minutes ago. 'Willow, I love you.' But she was gone. Taking his heart with her.

Where was her courage when she needed it more than ever? Willow swam hard and fast, ploughing the water with each determined stroke as she tried to leave Carter behind. It was as if he were following her, his image in her mind, relentlessly tormenting her.

All he'd asked of her was to talk. To explain her actions and needs. To help him understand her uncertainties. Not a lot given how well they got on. Too much considering how she had never talked in depth about what happened that day and how much it had hurt to lose her friends, her leg, and lastly Gavin because he couldn't deal with what had happened either.

Carter would cope. More than cope. He already understood her, knew when she needed help and when she didn't. Now she'd gone and hurt him badly. The pain had been there in his eyes, across his face, deepening his voice. All because she had lowered some of her barriers and let him in. But not far enough. Obviously he believed she was ready for something more than a fling. There were times she was, and then the doubts would return and she'd try to justify what she was doing by calling it a casual fling that would end at the same time as her contract finished.

Her contract had two weeks to go. Two weeks of hell having to work with Carter and pretend all was well in her world. She was never going to be the same again since knowing Carter. He'd shown her what was out there if she truly wanted it, was prepared to risk her heart and go for love. What she'd learned was that she was a coward, that protecting herself came before all else and she wasn't ready to let that go. That she was never likely to.

Sudden cramp seized her calf, forcing her to stop and roll onto her back. Massaging the muscles wasn't easy as she bobbed up and down in the sea. Pain stabbed every time she tried to stretch her leg. Massage, stretch, pain. Massage, stretch. Slowly the cramp relaxed until finally she began to breaststroke towards shore.

By the time she reached home she knew she'd be late to work, something she never was. Carter might think she'd skived off. As tempting as that was, she wouldn't do it. It was going to be hell working with him on the days he wasn't rostered to do the rural visits.

'Carter's swapped with Joe and will be on

rural duties all week,' Kathy told her with a concerned look when she dashed in the back door twenty minutes late.

'Oh.' Relief vied with deflation. If he'd been here she could hold onto some hope of being able to talk to him. But what was there to say? She'd had her chance last night and retreated fast. 'I'll get started, then. Sorry I'm late but I was out swimming and—' She stopped. Excuses weren't needed. 'I'm sorry,' she repeated and headed into the operating room where Joe had a puppy on the table.

The day dragged on for ever, as did the rest of the week. Nothing seemed to make the time go any faster and come Friday afternoon she couldn't get out of the clinic quick enough. There'd been no sign of Carter and she'd found herself tensing every time a door opened. It was never Carter who walked through. She had no one to blame but herself.

At the weekend she went away to Byron Bay, having never been there and thinking it would be the only opportunity she'd get to visit the art and crafts displays and spend some money on jewellery, which was her go-to for souvenirs. Earrings and bracelets were small and not cumbersome to cart around on her adventures.

In one gallery she stopped in front of a

painting of Main Beach in Southport. The sky was a searing blue and the sea lifted in small waves that spilled up the sand. Surfers and swimmers bobbed in the water… kids played in the sand. A dog ran along the water's edge. Her heart beat out of time as she stared at the painting, smelling the salt air, hearing the shrieks of children and the uncurling of the waves. It was as if she were right there, on the beach, feeling the water tickle her toes. A tear slipped down her cheek.

'Would you like to buy the painting?' asked a guy with dreadlocks and a soft smile. 'I can see you're smitten with it.'

The memories of walking the beach with Carter were roaring back, filling her with hope and love. Except the last time they were there they'd split up. 'No, thanks.' She tried to turn away, but her shoes were stuck to the floor.

'Maybe?'

She didn't need the memories it evoked, there were already too many crowding her head.

The last week working at the Southport clinic was much the same as the previous one. Carter was still working rurally, and Kathy

sometimes looked at her with a question in
her eyes, which she refused to acknowledge.
Walking out of the door for the last time was
harder than she'd expected. She'd brought
Axel in here, met Carter here, had a lot of
fun working here. Had lost her heart here.

Yes, she could finally admit to herself she
loved him, she thought as she trudged out to
her car for the final time.

'It's not too late to go and tell him,' said a
pesky voice in her head.

Yes, it was. She still couldn't guarantee
she wouldn't hurt Carter and that would be
as bad as being hurt herself. He deserved better. A lot better.

That night when she finally fell into a restless sleep she dreamed of Carter and Axel
and how easy they were to love. The dream
was followed with images of her flight docu-
ments and bags standing waiting at the door.
Then Dee flashed across her mind, followed
by Jess. They were shaking their heads at her
as if she'd been naughty and needed repri-
manding.

What? She sat up abruptly. Would Jess
and Dee think she should stay and take a
risk? How could they appear in her head?
They were gone, had no comprehension of
what had happened. Did they? No. Tossing

the cover aside, Willow headed for the bathroom and a long cool shower. She was the only one at home as her flatmates had gone to Melbourne for the weekend. She might as well call a cab and get on the road to the airport. Nothing to wait here for.

As she snipped the front door lock for the last time, her heart dragged. Usually it was beating with excitement at the prospect of a new place to see and people to meet. 'Auckland, here I come,' she muttered and hauled her bag down to the road to wait for the taxi.

CHAPTER NINE

'I'M NOT RENTING THIS,' Willow told the letting agent she'd contacted by email from Southport last month. She'd been in Auckland three days and needed to get accommodation sorted before she started work in ten days. 'It's a tip.' The walls and ceilings were black with mould, and there was an odour coming from the laundry she couldn't put her finger on but definitely wasn't a bunch of roses.

'You won't get anything else very quickly,' the agent told her. 'Nor as cheap.'

'Cheap?' She thought of the hundreds of dollars she was expected to pay weekly and shook her head. 'Forget it. I'm done.'

'I have to point out your deposit is non-refundable.'

She could fight that, but it would take energy she didn't have. She really didn't care. She just wanted out of here. 'Bye.' She headed for her rental car, still smelling that foul odour. A shower was next on her list of things to do. Which now included looking up other rental agencies and getting accommodation sorted fast.

Back at the hotel she extended her booking for another five days, and then had a shower before going for a walk along the Quay. She needed fresh air. Truly what she needed was to be walking along Main Beach, inhaling the warm salty air, and holding hands with Carter. Daydreaming was all very well, but so removed from reality it hurt. What she should be doing was getting on her phone and finding somewhere to live. She shrugged and ducked around a group of tourists admiring a superyacht tied up at the wharf. Urgent as it was, finding a flat could wait till tomorrow. Except she had an appointment to meet her new bosses tomorrow afternoon.

An appointment she missed because she got up in the morning and decided to take a ferry across to Waiheke Island, where she walked the beaches and ate lunch at a vineyard. By the time she returned to the central business district it was too late to get to the clinic before everyone left for the day, or so the vet who took her call to apologise told her.

'We'll set another time, and I'd appreciate it if you turned up.'

'Of course. I am sorry.' She'd never done something so random as forgetting an appointment with employers.

Over the coming days she visited Rangitoto Island, took a ferry across to Devonport where she managed to spend too many dollars on new boots and jeans. She drove to malls and outlying towns, walked through central Auckland, and often along the Quay where she ate at the various restaurants and cafes most days. She watched yachts racing on the Waitemata Harbour and visited One Tree Hill. She was doing what she always did when starting out in a new place, taking in the sights and learning the city layout, and getting excited to be there.

Except the excitement level was nil. Auckland was great, her sort of city with a buzzing centre and lots of things to do. And she couldn't raise a shred of enjoyment. Not one.

She was unhappy as she hadn't been before.

She missed Carter so much she ached non-stop.

On the day she made it to the clinic everyone was welcoming and quick to say it didn't matter she hadn't made it to the first appointment. *They must be desperate,* Willow thought as she followed Carol, the other vet nurse, around the building, learning where everything was. 'Is this a busy clinic?'

Carol paused in the middle of opening a cage to pet a cat. 'It's getting there.'

Three vets meant there needed to be a lot of animals coming through the doors to make ends meet, yet looking around at all the gleaming cages most were empty. Nothing like Rural And Suburban Veterinary Clinic. 'I suppose it's hard to start a new clinic in the middle of a CBD.'

'A lot of people living in downtown apartments have cats or dogs.'

She wondered where they were taking their pets, then, because it didn't look as though they were coming here. 'Early days.'

'That's what the bosses say,' Carol agreed, sounding worried.

'I wonder why the vets want me to start so soon.' It wasn't adding up. But neither was she feeling too bothered.

I don't want to be here.

The idea blasted at her. Shocked her.

'You'd have to ask them.' Carol straightened and shut the cage.

'What? Yes, of course. Sorry.'

I don't want to be here? Then where should I go?

How about Southport? There was a job going there she enjoyed. Abbie had not returned. Working alongside Carter when their fling was finished would be hell on steroids. Besides, they wouldn't take her back. Carter had done a disappearing act for the last two weeks she was at the clinic. He couldn't do that full time if she returned. The staff were his friends, they wouldn't want him upset by her returning.

He'd told her he wanted more with her, including getting to know what lay behind her fears and how they could work through those. When she hadn't reciprocated with a willingness to try to make it happen between them, he'd vanished from her life, at work and outside the clinic. She'd hurt him. She'd hurt herself. But she'd done the right thing in protecting herself. And Carter. Yes, because if she'd stayed, eventually she'd have walked away. This was how she lived. One city after another, one town to another. The safest way to go.

Except safe wasn't doing it for her. She was unhappy beyond belief. Since she'd already been in this state after the accident, it should feel familiar and acceptable. It didn't.

This was new. She loved Carter. Yes, she did, damn it. She'd never told him because then she'd be putting her heart out there to get smashed.

'What do you think of the clinic?' Carol asked.

Back to reality. 'It's like any other I've worked in except everything's brand new.'

'It will be good having you here. You'll know so much more than me. This is my first job as a vet nurse.'

Willow dug deep for a smile. 'It's an amazing job. I love dogs and getting to help them is great.'

Keep telling yourself that and eventually you might accept where you are.

Leaving the clinic, she walked along the Quay, tugging her jacket tight as the cool late autumn air felt damp and cold after the Gold Coast. She looked around at her new home town. Friday night and it was humming. The bars were busy, people were dashing here and there on the wide footpaths laughing and talking, and she felt a moment of intense pain. 'What are you doing, Carter?'

Halfway through the next week Willow parked in the underground park at the hotel after a day at Orewa, one of the city's top ten beaches. She had a thing about beaches since

Southport. So far none of them had come up to scratch. There was always something—someone—missing.

'Evening, Willow.' The girl behind the reception desk smiled as she made her way past. 'Where are you eating tonight?'

It had become a bit of a joke between them about where she ate her main meal of the day. Breakfast at the hotel, lunch could be a banana wherever she was, but she liked dinner to be something special. Spoiling herself for no reason other than she wanted to and needed to feel alive. 'I'll go back to the Italian on the Quay. Their linguini is to die for.'

'Found a flat yet?'

'No.'

'You been looking?'

'No.' She was a permanent hotel guest at the moment. Thank goodness for a solid bank account.

A frown creased the girl's forehead. 'Is everything all right?'

Let me see. I love a man who lives in Queensland. I miss him every breath I take. I'm not excited about this new adventure. I miss Carter. There was his upcoming thirtieth birthday party in June but she couldn't turn up for that now. Not and walk away again. It would be impossible.

'I guess.' She headed for the elevator before more disturbing thoughts came her way. She needed a coat if she was walking along the pier to the restaurant as the weather had turned blustery with a light drizzle.

As the elevator door swished shut, she gave a despondent sigh. It was time to get real. Stop being a sad sack. Put a smile on her face even if it hurt. She'd got into the doldrums and it was time to climb out.

'Enjoy dinner,' the concierge said as he held the door open for her ten minutes later.

'I will,' she replied, stepping out into the night lit with glowing streetlights and filled with the sounds of happy people. The envy had gone. She was responsible for her life. Those few minutes in the elevator had got her thinking beyond the ache in her heart. 'I have a plan.'

'Put some effort into it.' Cameron laughed at Carter. 'You're getting soft, man.'

'You reckon? Then how come I've dug eight holes while you've barely managed five? Who's the softie, eh?' Carter leaned on his shovel and looked around. They were nearly done with getting the holes ready for the framework to be laid for the foundations of a new shed behind their parents' house.

'Giving you a head start,' Cameron quipped. 'Townie brother needs toughening up.'

'Thought it was Carter who reined in your bucking bull the other day,' Calvin said to Cameron, adding his ten cents' worth to their banter.

Carter smiled. 'Cameron suddenly needed to see to the hens.' Brothers. Wouldn't be without them. They were there for the bad days as well as the good ones. There'd been a few bad ones since Willow left. Make that since she'd walked away from him on the beach, turning her back on his admission he wanted her more than anything and was prepared to risk his heart for her. Talk about knifing him where it hurt. Possibly not unexpected, but still painful. Had he gone too far too soon?

'That bull all right?' Calvin asked.

'Is now Carter got a thorn out of his male parts.'

They all looked at each other and started laughing. Better than squirming at the idea of a long sharp thorn in their testicles.

'Who'd be a vet, eh?'

'All in a day's work.' Carter tossed a shovelful of soil onto the trailer and wiped his brow. 'Dang, it's hot.' Autumn could still turn on some cracker days. He wondered what the temperatures were like in Auckland at the moment.

Cameron prodded him with his spade handle. 'Toughen up, old man. We'll be busy with this shed for weeks to come.'

'Here's the thing.' Carter straightened up. 'You'll have to manage without me next weekend. I'm heading to Auckland.' He had to give getting Willow to see how much he loved her another shot. It was all very well mulling over how she'd walked away, but he couldn't do the same so easily. She needed to see how much he cared and how he was prepared to stick by her as she got used to the idea of following her dreams and letting the past go. It was a risk, but if he didn't try then he only had himself to blame.

Calvin clapped him on the back. 'About bloody time. Had enough of that long face moping around the place.'

'Best idea you've had in a long while.' Cameron rammed his shovel into the soil.

So his brothers were backing him. He didn't expect any less but still. They made him feel better.

'Don't ask me to bring back any duty-free.' He grinned.

The sound of car wheels on the gravel

driveway caught his attention. 'Didn't think Ma was expecting anyone today.'

'Doesn't mean no one will turn up.'

True. His mother was social and well liked in the neighbourhood. Carter moved on to the next marker and began digging.

'Carter.' Calvin stood beside him. Cameron was coming across to join them. 'You've got a visitor.'

He turned slowly, his heart beginning to pound. His jaw dropped as he watched Willow walk across the yard towards him. Willow? She was meant to be in Auckland, not here.

She kept coming, no hesitation whatsoever. Those beautiful blue eyes were fixed on him, that sensual mouth halfway between smiling and tensing.

Was this good or bad? *Thump-thump* inside his chest.

Three metres away and she stopped, still looking at him. 'Hello, Carter.'

'Willow.'

'I've come home.'

Home? This wasn't her home. Wait up. What was she saying? She wanted to be with him?

'Meaning?' Blunt but all he was capable

of right now with a lump the size of Australia in his throat.

'I love you.' Her chest rose on those words. 'I love you, Carter.'

His head spun. His legs wobbled as he moved to reach her and take her hands in his and meet her unwavering gaze full on. 'I love you too, Willow. With all my heart.' About to haul her into his arms and kiss her, he hesitated. 'It's been hell these past weeks.'

'I am so sorry for how I reacted that night on the beach. I was wrong.'

'You were afraid.' As he was now. Afraid she'd have come to tell him they could never get together despite loving him.

'Yes, but so were you. I mean it when I say I love you. It took me a while to accept that I can't turn away from you. I don't want to. Ever.'

'Does that mean you'll move in with me? That we're a couple—for ever?' He had to know. Nothing else mattered.

'Absolutely.' Her smile widened. No sign of tension now.

His heart was leaping around inside his chest. 'Will you marry me? Have a family with me? Share whatever life throws our way?' His words were like a runaway train, nothing could halt them.

'Yes, Carter, I will.' Those gorgeous eyes were gleaming. 'Will you return the favour and marry me and have our babies and work through the ups and downs together?'

'Yes, Willow, I will. Come here.' He couldn't hold back any longer. He had to kiss her, to taste her, to feel her body against his. Had to.

It was a kiss like no other. It spoke of their love, their future, their *every*thing. It went on and on. He did not want to stop. When he finally lifted his head Willow was smiling so hard he knew everything would be all right.

Clapping broke into their solitude.

'Bravo.'

'About time.'

'Hurray.'

He groaned. 'Brothers. Who needs them?'

'We do.' Willow turned in his arms and beamed out at his family.

Yep, Mum and Dad were there too. Dad held a bottle of champagne, Mum the glasses, and his sisters-in-law were coming up behind them. He must've been kissing Willow for a long time, then. 'You'd better get used to this,' he groaned happily.

'You haven't met my family yet. They're going to get along so well.'

'Come on. Spill. What's going on?' Cameron demanded. 'Apart from the obvious. You've made up and think no one else knows how to kiss.'

'We're getting married.'

Dad sloshed the first glass of wine over the grass.

Mum dropped the rest of the glasses and raced towards them, threw her arms around Willow. 'Welcome home, darling. You have no idea how happy we are.'

Tears streamed down Willow's face. 'If it's anything like how I'm feeling, then I think I do.'

'Let's go to the house and get some more glasses,' Dad, the ever practical one, said.

'Before we join you I've got to take Willow to the barn. There's someone else who will be ecstatic to see her,' Carter said.

Sudden silence enveloped them.

Willow turned worried eyes on him. 'Who?'

Taking her hand, he pulled her along. 'Relax. It's all good.'

'Meet you at the house,' Calvin called.

Carter didn't pause. 'Right.' He was about to seal the deal with one more player in the picture.

'What's going on?' Willow asked as they rounded the barn.

Woof-woof.

She stumbled. 'Axel?'

He caught her and held her arm as he pulled the door wide. 'There you go.'

'Axel,' she shrieked. 'What are you doing here?'

The pup hurled himself at her, wagging so hard his tail was in danger of flying off.

'Mrs Burnside has gone into a retirement village where no large dogs are allowed. She asked if you might like to have him. There was no way was I letting him go anywhere else but here and hopefully to you.'

She was on her knees hugging Axel, tears streaming down her face. 'She didn't call me.'

'She lost all her contacts when her phone fell into the bath so she contacted me through the clinic.'

Clambering to her feet, Willow wrapped her arms around him and leaned back. 'This is the best day ever. I do so love you, Carter Adams. Yes, more than Axel. Just.' She smiled. Then leaned up for another kiss.

This time it didn't last as long because of a solid head nudging them in the thighs.

'The joys of having family, huh?' Willow patted Axel and grabbed Carter's hand. 'Let's go and celebrate with your family. And phone mine with the good news.'

'They can join in the fun on Zoom.'

They were both smiling as they returned to the house. Before taking her inside, Carter paused and leaned in for another kiss. 'I can cancel my ticket to Auckland now.'

'What?'

'I was going over next weekend to ask you for a second chance. There was no way you were leaving me that easily. I love you too much.'

Her tears only got more insistent. 'Back at you,' she whispered, then kissed him senseless.

* * * * *